D0016502

A Blind Corner

ALSO BY CAITLIN MACY

Mrs.

Spoiled

The Fundamentals of Play

A Blind Corner

Stories

CAITLIN MACY

Little, Brown and Company

New York   Boston   London

The characters and events in this book are fictitious. Any similarity to real persons, living or dead, is coincidental and not intended by the author.

Copyright © 2022 by Caitlin Macy

Hachette Book Group supports the right to free expression and the value of copyright. The purpose of copyright is to encourage writers and artists to produce the creative works that enrich our culture.

The scanning, uploading, and distribution of this book without permission is a theft of the author's intellectual property. If you would like permission to use material from the book (other than for review purposes), please contact permissions@hbgusa.com. Thank you for your support of the author's rights.

Little, Brown and Company
Hachette Book Group
1290 Avenue of the Americas, New York, NY 10104
littlebrown.com

First Edition: June 2022

Little, Brown and Company is a division of Hachette Book Group, Inc. The Little, Brown name and logo are trademarks of Hachette Book Group, Inc.

The publisher is not responsible for websites (or their content) that are not owned by the publisher.

The Hachette Speakers Bureau provides a wide range of authors for speaking events. To find out more, go to hachettespeakersbureau.com or call (866) 376-6591.

ISBN 9780316434195
LCCN 2021949982

Printing 1, 2022

LSC-C

Printed in the United States of America

For Jeremy
and Jem

Contents

A Blind Corner

One of Us

The Gearys had plans with Frances's mother for Memorial Day, and the next weekend Ted's firm had its corporate picnic, so they didn't take possession of the rental cottage till the second Saturday in June. Their nearest neighbors, Annie and Tom Ziegler, were also their landlords. The weekend after the Gearys moved in, the Zieglers had a dinner party so that they could meet people. "Gotta initiate the newbies!" said Tommy Ziegler when he caught Ted buying a quart of milk in Cullen's, the general store. He clapped him on the back. "Leicester tradition."

A hundred miles from the city, the town of Leicester was less well known than other nearby towns where city people rented. Frances had chosen it for that very reason after trying and rejecting more popular towns in previous summers. Lucas was nearly two now. They were anxious to establish themselves somewhere—to start piling up those idyllic memories neither Frances nor Ted had had the privilege to enjoy as children.

When Ted, returning with the quart of milk, told Frances they were invited to the Zieglers' for dinner, she was pleased and a little bit excited. "Did you hear that, Lucas?" she said to the toddler sitting in the high chair as she cut up toast for him in the cottage's funny old kitchen with the coffee percolator and the three-quarter-size pull-door fridge. "Mommy and Daddy are already making friends in Leicester!"

"Oh, jeez!" Ted called back through the screen door as he went to get his bicycle out of the shed. "Remind me to get a printout of the lease and sign it!"

"We haven't signed the lease?" Frances said worriedly. Late in the spring she had driven up from the city and found the place. Ted had said he would deal with the paperwork.

"We sent them a check last month! I just kept forgetting to mail the thing!"

Taking Lucas for a walk in the stroller that afternoon Frances caught Annie Ziegler outside her house, weeding her flower beds. Though she had crow's-feet and a weathered face, Frances's landlord wore her hair in two braids, like a little girl. She sat back on her heels, trowel in hand, and waved away Frances's apology about the lease. "Please—no worries, Frances! No worries at all!" She spoke in a quiet, silvery voice that sent shivers down Frances's spine.

"So who'll be there tonight?" Frances asked genially.

"Oh, you know..." Annie waggled her fingers at Lucas. "The usual suspects."

Frances had already put Lucas to bed when the babysitter arrived—a reticent older woman from town called Mrs. Deans. Frances showed her in and went to finish getting ready. She looked critically at herself in the old, de-silvered mirror above the ramshackle chest of drawers. The chest, like most of the furniture in the cottage, had been perked up with a coat of white paint. Touching her string of beads with her fingertips, Frances felt unhappy, wondering how she and Ted would measure up. Ted could be difficult. Reticent by nature, he would suddenly speak up at the most inopportune moments. And he didn't suffer fools. When he emerged from the shower, Frances watched him in the mirror toweling off. After a moment, she said irritably, "Can you please, please make an effort tonight? Can you please not judge everyone right off the bat? Can you please just go along to get along?" She looked back at her reflection and frowned, then tried a smile and turned her head from side to side. "I wonder what she'll serve. I wonder if they'll drink...God, I hope it's not like Grenville. I hope it's not a huge bore."

"I hope you like rosé!" she said unctuously to Annie Ziegler half an hour later, handing over a bottle of wine. She was in apologetic mode because, after walking the fifty yards of cracked, country hardtop that separated the cottage from the Zieglers' main house, she and Ted had gone to the wrong door—the front door, which had to be unlocked in three places and pried open amid clouds of dust—rather than the side door that everyone else had known to use.

"It's not expensive, but Ted and I love it."

"That is so thoughtful of you, Frances!" Annie beamed. "*So* thoughtful. *Thank* you! And you too, Ted. Now, Ted, you go on out to the porch—just follow the noise—and Frances, you come with me. Come meet the gals."

As Frances was led away to the kitchen, she glanced back at Ted and gave him a meaningful look. Ted held up both hands with his fingers crossed—being facetious. *Be nice!* she mouthed, and tried to look severe.

In the kitchen, three women were standing around an island beneath a pot rack, big goblets of wine in their hands. The kitchen had been renovated in that anodyne, any-town style of glass, apothecary-type cabinets and marble counters. The first thing Frances noticed, as the women turned with what looked to be a mixture of curiosity and welcome, was that one of them was old enough to be her mother. As Annie introduced Pam Carmichael and Theresa Dowe and Pilar—who had a complicated surname involving *de*—Frances concentrated very hard, repeating the names to herself: *Pam Theresa Pilar, Pam Theresa Pilar.* She was reading a book on improving one's memory, and immediate repetition was one of the author's tips. *Pam Theresa Pilar, Pam Theresa Pilar.* "Now, Theresa's in the city during the week like you and me," Annie went on, pointing. "Pilar and Felipe moved back to Argentina two years ago, but, if you can believe it, they still make the pilgrimage to little ol' Leicester in the summers! And Pam used to be in the city, but she and Chappie retired up here, so now they're year-rounders."

"Oh—how great," said Frances. "I'd love to move to the country!"

"Would not we all?" said Pilar with a jokey grimace. She was a tall, striking woman of about forty, with dark hair pulled back into a twist. She wore a colorful cotton dress and spoke English slowly and with an intriguing accent—later on, Frances found out she was Spanish, from Madrid; her husband was Argentinean. "Too bad some of us have to hold down the job!"

"You're so right!" Frances said quickly, and "I'll have white—thank you!" when Annie held up two bottles of wine. She gulped quickly at the glass she was given, feeling unaccountably nervous. "Whenever I say I want to leave the city, Ted says, 'And what would I do for a living, pray tell?'" She laughed. "*I* quit when we had the baby, so I really can't talk."

This set off a flurry of interest, warm and encouraging.

"How old?"

"Aw, that's a great age."

"Ees it a boy or a girl?" asked Pilar. Only Theresa Dowe stayed silent—standing back and observing the exchange with a sardonic look on her face that made Frances blanch. *Oh God, what did you do this time?* she could hear Ted asking her at the end of the night. *Nothing!* Frances made her imaginary protest. *I swear!*

"It's true what they say, Frances—the hours and days drag," Annie Ziegler opined softly.

"But the years," the older woman broke in, "they just fly, don't they?" This was Pam. *Pam Carmichael. Preppy Pam,* Frances thought. Another technique the memory book had suggested was putting a descriptive epithet with a name. "Trust me—they go like that!" Pam snapped her fingers. "Y'all are sitting there telling bedtime stories and then, boom, it's off to college!"

Frances smiled gratefully. Pam was a bosomy brunette, dressed in that tailored style that evokes the Reagan era. She wore a polo shirt and loud pants and tended to a wicker purse on the counter in front of her. Frances quickly assessed that Pam wasn't the kind of person she would have naturally befriended in the city. There was the age difference, and no doubt she would turn out to be politically conservative. But Frances had a contrarian streak—it had brought her to Leicester in the first place—and she had a soft spot for the South, having lived there briefly; Pam's *y'all* took her back to that sunny, carefree year after college when she had lived in a group house and worked at a menial job. She was beyond tired of their crowd in the city. She was fed up to here with the "urban liberal clusterfuck," as she put it—bored silly by her and Ted's peers' predictable pretensions and child-brilliance one-upmanship: *Miles is finishing his opera in his spare time. Stella has taught herself Sanskrit.*

"It's not Dowe anymore," Theresa was saying testily to Annie. "I told you, I went back to my maiden name. It's Perkins. I go by Perkins now."

"In Madrid it is not really done—for a woman to change her name," observed Pilar.

"Gosh, I been Carmichael so long," Pam said cozily, "I wouldn't know myself as Pam Blanchard."

Frances smiled doggedly but felt a prick of despair when she stole a glance at dour Theresa. She had barely arrived in Leicester, and yet the one woman who was exactly her age seemed to have taken against her. Any awkwardness, though, was covered up by a roar of laughter from the porch. "Come on! Let's go eat before they get too drunk!" said Annie.

"Who, them?" Pam said dryly, and the others laughed.

As the women made their way through the living room, the back strap of Frances's sandal fell down, and she knelt to tighten it. "Here, let me hold that." Annie relieved Frances of her glass of wine. She leaned over and murmured, "Don't worry about Theresa. She's just bitter about her divorce."

"Um, er…Theresa?" Frances straightened up, unable to think of how to respond to this.

"In the jeans and the blouse?" Annie said. "Her husband dumped her and ran off with his secretary. Three little kids at home. So she's kinda hating life these days. Once she gets to know you, though, there's not a more loyal friend in the world." Annie handed back Frances's glass of wine. "So, who do you have babysitting tonight?" When Frances told her, Annie stopped short and shook her head. "Oh, dear God—Shirley Deans. Bless you, Frances. She's still at it. With her little index card in Cullen's..."

"She's okay, isn't she?" Frances said anxiously. "I mean, she's all right—right?"

Annie made a dismissive gesture. "She's fine—she's totally fine. Once there was a—not exactly an incident...you can ask Pilar."

Frances found she was shaking. She stood, paralyzed, in the dim hallway that led to the porch. "Oh my God. I just—I didn't know anyone! She had so many references! Should I go home?" she asked Annie. "Do I need to leave?"

"No, no, no! Oh God—I'm not being clear!" Annie gave Frances's shoulder an encouraging squeeze. "She's *fine* at night when the kids are asleep. She's absolutely fine. Responsible—whatever. It's just—" She hesitated. "She likes to discipline them. Even the little ones."

"What?"

"Frances, we *all* used her. She's the only game in town! Or was. But you know what? Here's what you do." Annie moved her face in close to Frances's, as if to make sure she was paying attention. "You tell her when you get back tonight that for the rest of the summer, Tara Ziegler is babysitting for you."

"Your daughter?" Frances was so grateful and relieved, her voice cracked.

"My one and only." Annie's smile was warm and empathetic. "How easy is that, right? You won't even have to drive her home. She loves kids, and she *loves* babies and toddlers. Just super-maternal, my Tara. And she'll play with him and everything, not just sit there on her phone like some of these kids."

"Oh, that would be great!" Frances swallowed. "Would it be too weird if—I mean, is it okay if I text her right now?"

Annie shrugged. "Sure! She's over at Neal's—her boyfriend's. Go ahead."

The two women got their phones out, and Annie shared her daughter's contact. It didn't work at first; they had to step back into the living room to get service. "Leicester all the way," said Annie. "We're in our own private Idaho here, I'm telling you."

"I can give her regular work!" Frances said. "Please tell her— a few hours every afternoon, and nights! Here. I'm writing it right here: 'I would like to hire you . . .' A couple nights a week! At least, Annie! I mean—I'd love to sew her up if I can! It can be so hard in towns where you're new . . ."

"You don't know who to trust!" Annie concurred as they went out onto the porch finally.

"Oh, look—she already texted me back! God, I can't thank you enough."

Annie put up a hand. "Please! Leicester's like this—we help each other out."

Frances was still so shaken that she took a second to get her bearings on the screened porch and drank what was left in her glass. Her eyes sought Ted's, but he didn't look her way. He was holding a drink and standing between their host, Tommy Ziegler, and another, older man who was meticulously clean-shaven in a jacket and bow tie with his hair slicked down. This must be Pam Carmichael's husband. Ted looked very serious—alarmingly serious. Frances felt a pang of fear, but then he laughed, throwing his head back—"Ha-ha! That's a good one!"—and she let out a breath. Now she could relax.

The nine adults sat at a long table that almost filled the screened porch. Frances had to mince around the corner of the table to squeeze herself down into her seat. She loved that the Zieglers were game to mush in as many guests as they could. As the others came to the table, it was all very cheerful but in the low-key, almost professional way of people who socialize together a lot. The table was covered in a blue print tablecloth but set with paper plates. Frances liked that too—the lack of pretension spoke directly to some cherished part of herself that she'd had to bury, occupied as she and Ted had been these last several years with the getting and spending, the relentless push toward advancement and the jockeying for position that living in the city entailed.

"Annie always uses paper plates," Pam Carmichael explained to Frances from across the table as she settled her wineglass at her place and then herself in her chair. Tommy courteously stood behind the older woman to push her in—"Here you go, Pammie"—then went outside to the deck to tend a gas grill. "It's her thing," Pam said.

"That's right," said Annie, standing at the foot of the table. "And I always serve the same thing, don't I? Don't I?" she repeated, tapping on her glass with a knife.

"Steak, baked potatoes, and a green salad," recited the others as the stragglers—Pilar and her husband, who had been sharing a cigarette outside next to the grill—came to the table. "Feelsy habit—just feelsy," said Pilar. "I apologize for my bad manners."

Annie introduced Frances to the men and Ted to the women. Every time she used Frances's name—which she did frequently, in that kindly, hyper-inclusive way Frances associated with yoga teachers—Frances felt prickles on the back of her neck. "Now, Frances…"; "I want to make sure, Frances…" Pilar's husband, Felipe, took the seat diagonally across from her. The Argentine had a dark fall of hair over his forehead and wore a sweater tied around his shoulders, European-style. He removed it and hung it carefully on the back of his chair. "It ees wonderful to meet you," he said, locking eyes with Frances, who flushed and had to look away.

Tommy Ziegler banged through the screen door with a platter of meat. "Got a rare one for you, Felipe—you can see where the jockey hit it!"

Amid laughter, a voice called out, "Everyone good for drinks?" This was Chappie Carmichael, the man in the bow tie and jacket. He was standing in front of a low drinks table— a card table with a gingham cloth over it—that had been set up by the door. "I already made yours, Pammie."

"Aw, thanks, babe!" Pam turned back to the table. "Love my Chappie."

"I could use another!" someone down the table piped up. It was Ted. Frances looked at him in alarm. He was doing exactly as she'd asked—he was being polite; he was being affable, even, and sociable, which went against his nature. In order to do that, she realized, he was having to get lubricated.

"What was that, Ted? G and T?"

"That's right! G and T-T-T it is!" The two of them guffawed as Ted half stood and passed his glass to Chappie, apparently at some inside joke already established between them. Frances crushed her napkin against her thigh under the table. There was nothing she could do. She would just have to hope he didn't get so drunk that he did something stupid and ruinous. She pasted on the most ingratiating smile she could muster. She was willing to work overtime, do anything she could to make this happen. She just couldn't face starting over in a new town—not again. Having to find out where the farmers' market was and how to get a dock sticker...

Annie had gone on explaining, for Frances's benefit, her evolution to paper plates and a set menu, which made entertaining easier.

"And the rest is history!" cried Chappie. He delivered Ted's drink and came around and squeezed himself between Frances and Theresa.

"We been sittin' here ever since!" Pam chimed in eagerly.

"To history!" Annie said in her whispery voice that made you lean in to catch every word.

"To history!"

"No matter how it fucks with us," muttered Theresa grimly.

Frances died a little inside as she raised her glass because, of course, she and Ted had had no part in this Leicester history. She wasn't naive, though. She understood that this was the price of joining any established group. She tried to look plucky and interested and not to mind as she clinked glasses with everyone near her—Chappie, Tommy, at the head of the table to her left, Felipe, and Pam.

13

Platters of steak and baked potatoes began to circulate. "This all looks great!" Ted cried. "This—!"

"Butter?" Frances said firmly, offering it to Tommy, who took it absently, without making eye contact. Their host, whom people called TZ, was a large, diffident man—sweating in his shirtsleeves, careful not to let their elbows touch. "Damn it, Annie, it's hot in here!"

Frances was trying to think of a suitable topic of conversation when TZ suddenly banged the table with his fists, fork in one hand, knife in the other, and yelled, "That had nothing to do with it, Chap! I was making seventy-five thousand dollars a year and had so much debt—Leicester was the only town I could *afford!*" He speared a bite of steak.

Ted's voice rang out across the table over the laughter. "Well, which route out of the city do you guys take?"

Tommy Ziegler said cheerfully, his mouth full, "Now, *that* is a matter of some debate, Teddy, my man. How much time you got?"

Chappie Carmichael's hand shook, Frances noticed, as he raised the tumbler of gin to his mouth. "You're not gonna argue for Three Twenty-Three to Nine, Tom, you're just not." *Jutht not.* Already there was a slur to his words. He had the slicked-down hair and careful shave of someone who was trying to keep it together. Was he a bona fide alcoholic? Frances tried not to stare. But as she looked away, a sense of indignant protectiveness of Chappie rose up in her. The urban clusterfuck were all so goddamned controlled and controlling—they were always giving up dairy or running an ultramarathon or boring you to death with their vegan or paleo or Ayurvedic regimens. Her best momfriend had crowed to her that she had ketones in her urine!

"As the crow flies—" Tommy began.

"As the crow flies bullshit! There's a cop every ten miles on Route Nine. Don't listen to him, Ted! What you wanna do is—"

Frances stole a glance across the table at the handsome Felipe. He was encouraging Annie to make a trip to Buenos Aires this winter, but he suddenly looked deeply into Frances's eyes as if they were alone in the room. "And you must come to BA too, of course," he said. Frances gave a wan smile and reached for her glass but found it empty. She tipped nothing but air down her throat.

"Well, that went fast," said Tommy Ziegler beside her. "Kidding! Kidding," he added when Frances opened her mouth in surprise. "You can take a joke, right? See, I don't have these fancy manners some people have. I wasn't born with a silver spoon in my mouth."

"Oh, me either!" said Frances, glad to be given this conversational opening.

"Like Chappie Carmichael, for instance!" shouted Tommy. He still did not make eye contact with Frances but talked urgently out of the side of his mouth in a low voice, for her ears only. "Everything I have"—he waved toward the fences and the fields beyond the screened porch—"I earned. I grew up poor—like, *poor*-poor, you got me? Love these kids who say they grew up poor, and it turns out what they mean is they never skied in Europe, know what I mean?"

"I *do!*" Frances leaned toward him in an effort to convey her sincerity. "I really and truly do! That's Ted's and my whole *thing*. Ted's the son of a single mother and I—I was the poster child for financial aid!" Another thing, she thought peevishly, that the clusterfuck didn't have a clue about, didn't understand at all. If one more person told her, "Well, our parents gave us the down payment..." or "I inherited a small portfolio of mutual funds..."

"I'm talking food-stamps poor," Tommy said. "I'm a redneck, okay? *I* can say that about myself." He pushed his chair back, got up, and went down the other side of the table with a bottle of red wine, filling glasses. "Not like Mr. Chapman Carmichael! Chappie here never worked a day in his life! Or, no, wait—what did you do in college again, Chap? Weren't you a lifeguard at some posh country club?"

Chappie chuckled as Tommy finished by filling Frances's glass, ignoring her protest of "Oh, I had white...well, maybe just a half..."

"Caddie."

"*Caddie,* he says!" barked Tommy. "Driving a golf cart from hole to hole while I *broke rocks* in a quarry! While I worked in a desiccant factory! You know what desiccant is, Frances? It's the little packet they put in your vitamins to keep 'em dry."

"Yes, TZ. We *know!*" Annie rolled her eyes.

"Fucking know that, TZ," grumbled Theresa. "You've told us a hundred fucking times."

The volume at the long table rose and rose. Pilar sang a ditty in Spanish that apparently had erotic overtones.

"Fucking bullshit!" Theresa spit out in response to something someone had said.

"Y'all are too serious for me!" Pam cried. "And too smart! Ted, you are *really* smart, I can tell. Now, what is it that y'all do when you're not entertaining older women?"

Ted made a joke about the legal profession, his delivery perfect.

As the platter of steak went around for seconds, Chappie regaled Frances with tales of Leicester. "Let me tell you, Frances, about the Time It Snowed in October and TZ Had to Plow Everyone Out," said the older man. It was as if he'd been turned on—mechanically, not sexually—and could not stop till he wound down. "Let me tell you about the Time the Liquor Store Closed Early and We Had a 'Stone Soup' Cocktail Party—"

"Chappie brought the peppermint—what you call it—the peppermint schnapps!" Pilar interrupted.

"It was all we had!" protested Chappie.

Frances laughed at the punch lines, not uncharmed, and looked carefully around the table. Felipe's stare had become so intense, she was relieved when he excused himself to go have another cigarette. Chappie was halfway through the Time Bruno (the Dog) Ate the Turkey before it dawned on Frances that he was referring to Thanksgiving.

These people weren't just acquaintances, of course—she had sensed that right away. But now she knew the whole of it. Maybe it was the wine, but when she was faced with the incontrovertible truth, it made her feel forlorn and left out: these people spent their holidays together. Appallingly, tears threatened. "Something in my contact—I'm sorry—bathroom." Mumbling, she rose and got awkwardly out from the tight side of the table.

The door down the hall that Annie directed her to was shut; there seemed to be someone inside, but Frances didn't even bother to try the knob to make sure. She just stood in the dark hall and closed her eyes, trying not to cry. They would never belong anywhere, she and Ted. Like sinners in some summer-colony religion, they seemed predestined never to belong, as if there were something about them that had branded them with outsider status for the rest of their lives. Some air of desperation or neediness, or maybe it was just her hypercritical mindset. Lucas would have no friends and be consigned to a life of solitude and paranoia, just like her.

"Are you all right?" Frances snapped open her eyes as the door creaked open. Felipe was standing right in her personal space. He looked at her with concern. She could barely breathe. He was so sexually attractive, she could have knelt down right there and then and given him a blow job. Instead, she looked vaguely up—vaguely away from him.

"I am going to have another cigarette. Would you like to join me, Frances?"

"Oh—no. No, thank you. I don't smoke. I mean, I have smoked, I'm not one of these anti-smoking Nazis..."

He listened, his face unmoving. His self-possession—his quietude—made Frances tremble. *American men!* she thought with aggrieved exasperation. The whole goddamn clusterfuck going on about their techniques for brining, for sourdough starters; comparing notes on the jamminess of their favorite pinot noir. Whereas Felipe—Felipe took her face in his hands and flicked his thumb gently over her cheekbone. "If you change your mind..."

Frances staggered into the bathroom. She shut the door and felt her face where he had touched it. She mugged and grinned at herself in the mirror. She sat on the toilet shaking her head, then just laughing. And she had worried the evening would be a bore! The one thing she had never thought of in these years of social mobility was having an affair. She had been pregnant, nursing...she had been too busy, too tired, too irritated, too anxious...but now in Leicester! Leicester, of all places.

When she opened the door, Ted was standing there.

"You looked so upset, hon—I just wanted to make sure you were okay."

"Yeah, I just got—I don't know." She no longer minded about anything and so was able to speak lightly, in a voice imbued with good humor. "I fucking hate starting over, you know? I feel like we'll never be accepted anywhere and we're just going to be, like, these *journeymen*...I don't want to keep trying new towns every summer! It's depressing!"

"We're not going anywhere," Ted said with uncharacteristic authority.

"What do you mean?" Frances said. "How can you be so sure?"

Ted glanced behind him, and his voice dropped to a murmur. "You know the Miradox litigation? The arthritis thing?"

"Of course I know the Miradox litigation!" Frances whispered hotly. "I do listen when you talk about work, despite what you think!" It was only the enormous class-action defense Ted's firm had been pitching to try and get for six months.

"Yeah? Yeah?" He laughed rather maniacally.

"Ted! Stop!" she hissed. "You sound hysterical. Are you drunk?"

"Okay, so our landlord and host, Thomas A. Ziegler, is head of compliance for the people who make that shit."

"Oh my God, Ted." She stared at him. "You're kidding me. You are fucking kidding me."

Ted shook his head. "Indeed I am not, my lady."

"Oh my God!" she murmured. "Oh. My. God."

"I bring this in? I'm gonna make partner. You realize that, right?"

"The karma in this place! It's just—it's crazy. It's unbeliev-able!" She added quickly, "And we fucking deserve it. After those assholes last summer? 'There's a ten-year waiting list and even then . . .' You know what? Take your waiting list and shove it up your ass!"

"I know." Ted tottered, off balance, then lurched by her and into the bathroom. "I'm fine! I'm totally fine," he said, putting up a hand as he steadied himself on the vanity.

"Ted, you're wasted! Please," Frances pleaded. "Please, just be careful, okay? I don't want to fuck it up. Think about Miradox!" she begged.

"I'm fine!" he half shouted as Pam Carmichael went by, empty platters in her hands.

"He's fine, ha-ha!" Frances said.

"Well, I should hope so!" said Pam. "Chappie makes a mean G and T!"

Ted had closed the bathroom door. Frances rapped quietly on it. "You okay, Ted?" she murmured. "You sure you're okay?"

"I'm fine—I'm fine, Frannie. I just gotta—I gotta get it together. I'll be right out, I promise you, right out."

Pam reappeared and Frances followed her back to the table, chatting volubly, not wanting to draw attention to Ted's absence. Chappie was standing at the little drinks table fixing himself another, and Tommy Ziegler was engaged in what looked to be a serious conversation with Felipe, but he stopped and opened his arm to gesture her back as she took her seat.

"So what do you say, Frances?" said that warm, silvery-soft voice.

It took Frances a moment to find Annie Ziegler at the other end of the table. "Wait, what do I say? You mean, do I—"

Pam gave a giggle. "Y'all in or out?"

"In or out?" Frances was embarrassed because she didn't get the joke. "I'm sorry," she said miserably. "Did I miss something?"

Chappie sipped off the top of his fresh drink. "Thanksgiving! It's only five months away!"

TZ clapped her on the back. "Poor kid—she's probably dying to get the hell out of here and never come back, but she's too polite to say so! Ha-ha-ha!"

"Will you be joining the Leicester crew?" Pilar inquired. "Tragically, Felipe and I can no longer come. It is too far from Buenos Aires, and it is not a holiday in Argentina. Our 'Turkey Days' are behind us."

"Me?" Frances said wondrously.

"Well..." Pam paused, her eyes twinkling. "I think we'll let ol' Ted come too!"

Frances wished she could roll with it, but she couldn't even manage to smile. "But you don't even know us! I mean—you just met us!" She looked around the table at the cheerful, attentive expressions. "How do you know we're not awful?"

"I can assure you—we're not awful!" Ted joked, appearing from the bathroom and walking unsteadily to his chair.

Annie didn't falter. "I just know, Frances," she said. Her eyes were bright. "I can always tell."

Squeezing back in beside her, Chappie said, "Some people get Leicester. Some people don't."

TZ pretended to cough as he said, "The Johnsons!"

"Oh God—don't remind us," someone said.

"Oh, dear—what did the Johnsons do?" Frances asked, feeling an enjoyable rush of schadenfreude.

Even grim Theresa was nodding, a look of acceptance softening her harsh, dismissive mien. "I knew you were gonna fit in. Didn't I say to you, Annie? When we watched them walking up to the wrong door earlier? I said, 'That doesn't matter because they're the kind of people we like.'"

Frances blinked rapidly. For the second time that night, she was afraid she was going to cry. "We—I mean, both of us," she said, including Ted in a gesture, "we'd love to." She knew she sounded too serious, as if it mattered too much, as if this were the invitation she had been pathetically waiting for her whole life. She prayed they couldn't detect the tremor in her voice when she said, "I just hope the dog doesn't eat the turkey this year!"

Approving laughter spun them into the dessert course—strawberries and whipped cream. Frances tried to get up to help dish it out, but Pam waved her down. "That side of the table never helps. It's too hard to get out. Y'all just sit there and hold down the fort."

"Look what I did," said Annie, returning from the kitchen with a French press pot of coffee and a piece of paper. "I printed out the lease for you."

"Oh my God, Annie, thank you so much! We tried to get it done in town but—"

"Yeah, good luck with that!" said Theresa.

"*Magnífico!*" cried Ted, who had hauled out his high-school Spanish to converse with Pilar. Chappie withdrew a pen from his breast pocket. Ted signed with a flourish and then Frances did, happy and relieved, as she didn't want Annie to think they were taking things for granted or presuming that their nascent friendship meant that they wouldn't respect the fiscal relationship.

Annie glanced at it and then up at Ted and Frances, grinning. "Did you notice I changed the term? Instead of Labor Day, I put a year." She held up a hand. "Same price! Same price! It's not *about* the money."

"What?"

"Really? Are you sure, Annie?"

"*Un año!*" cried Ted. "*Perfecto!* I mean, if we're gonna be here for Thanksgiving, right? Which is great by me! My brother's wife is a fucking control freak!" With a violent lurch, Ted pushed himself up from the table and made for the hallway. *Jesus, Ted!* Frances thought, gritting her teeth. He was going to throw up, she was sure of it.

"Easy does it there, Teddy boy!" Chappie chuckled. Behind Frances, their chairs pushed back, he and TZ continued their political conversation as if they'd hardly noticed the state Ted was in. Frances just tried to smile and make small talk to cover his behavior. Annie Ziegler left briefly and returned carrying a little silver tray with cream and sugar on it. She set it down in the middle of the table. "Ted's passed out on the couch," she announced.

"Oh no!" cried Frances, mortified. "I'm so sorry! God, I'm sorry, Annie! Work has been insane...I think he was just psyched to unwind—"

Annie gave Frances a withering look. "You think every one of us seated at this table haven't all gotten so wasted we

23

couldn't see straight? A hundred times? That's what friends are for!"

"I am European. We don't get 'wasted' the way you do in America," Pilar observed. "We have a small glass, perhaps a vermouth. A glass of sherry..."

Pam leaned across the table and put a warm hand over Frances's. "Y'all *really* don't have to worry—that's the beauty of Leicester." She squeezed Frances's hand as she made her point. "No one will ever judge you here. For anything. *Anything.* You're one of us, ya hear?"

Frances nodded, humbled by the sentiment.

"Anyway," Theresa said dryly from her end of the table, "nothing TZ hates more than a teetotaler!"

"Is that true?" Frances turned to her, dropping all pretension. "Is that really true? All right, well—thank you. All of you." She tried to smile as she dug into her berries and cream. "These guys work so hard...I guess we've been a little stressed. I don't know—toddler, new town." She turned to Theresa. "So, you're in human resources?" This much Frances had gathered at some point. Too late, she realized she didn't have a single intelligent follow-up question to ask about Theresa's job, so she just cleared her throat and said determinedly, "What's that like?"

"These days?" Theresa raised her eyebrows. "A lotta bullshit. Trying to hire URMs, that kinda crap."

"UR—sorry?"

Listening in, TZ put his hands up to make air quotes. "'Under. Represented. Minorities.' Load of crap." He said to Frances, "Did it ever occur to you that maybe they're underrepresented 'cause they're not qualified?"

"Uh, *yeah*," Theresa said rudely. "It did occur to me, TZ—that's my whole fucking point."

"I grew up poor!" Tommy said. "Food-stamps poor—you with me? My dad had a stroke when I was fourteen and never worked again. You don't see me expecting a handout, do you, Frances? You don't see me thinking someone should just give me a job on a silver plate, do you?" He went back to his debate with Chappie.

Pilar spoke up. "If I may ask you, Frances, do you feel safe in the city with a small child?"

"Safe?" Frances said distractedly. "Sure. I mean, it can be a hassle. Schlepping the stroller everywhere…"

"Do not get me wrong. I *love* the city. I absolutely love it. I say to Felipe every day: 'Please! Let us move back! I am begging you! Let us move back to America.' But after dark…" She and Theresa exchanged glances. "The *animals* come out!"

"Animals?" Frances said, recalling an incident when Ted had been confronted by a pair of raccoons in the park at night.

"You know what I mean, the ones who come out to prowl!"

"Crime rates have dropped in the city, Pilar," TZ said judiciously. "Crime's way down since you and Felipe left." He tipped his chair back to continue his conversation with Chappie.

Pilar gave an elaborate shrug. "Perhaps. If it were I…"

Annie hovered nearby with the coffeepot. "So, are you gonna be up in Leicester full-time with that cutie-patootie little Lucas for the summer and Ted'll go back and forth?"

"I—"

Annie beamed. "Super. Just super. Hey, Tom! Tommy! You know what I'm thinking about for the next dinner party?"

"Annie, I'm having a serious conversation here. Can you please not interrupt me?"

Well, excuuuuuuse me, Annie mouthed to Frances. "Cream, anyone? Sugar? Who takes sugar?"

"Kenyan in the fucking White House!" TZ said insistently. "What do you expect?"

"That's not my point—"

"They get to feeling empowered. That's all I'm saying. They get to feeling empowered."

"Sure, given. But that's not my point, TZ—"

"Did I ever tell you ladies about the time I was mugged in broad daylight? These *animals* came after me. They got everything! They took my watch! It was a present from Felipe for our anniversary."

Pam murmured something to Pilar.

Pilar looked exasperated. "What do you think, Pam?"

"Can't say *Black*, Pammie!" Theresa interjected loudly. "It's *African-American*. They don't want to be called *Black* anymore." She gave a bark of laughter. "That was last year."

"Oh, Pilar," Annie was saying softly. "That is terrible. I am so sorry. I am so very sorry for your trauma."

"'Twas indeed traumatic. They surrounded me. One—he was threatening me, swearing, you know?"

"Motherfuckah!" Theresa cackled.

TZ let the front legs of his chair drop to the floor and picked up a fresh bottle of red. "So, Frances, we never told you the best story about Leicester."

"No, thank you!" Frances said. She shifted her wineglass away from him.

"Just a little taste," TZ insisted. "Finish what you've got in your glass—this is the good stuff. We saved the best for last! South African cabernet. Okay, so I call this one 'When the Johnsons Came to Town.'"

"Oh, no, Tommy." Frances shook her head. "I don't want to hear that one."

"Nah, nah—you gotta hear it. It's a funny one. It's really fucking funny."

"I can guess how it ends, Tommy!"

"You can?" Tommy looked miffed. He shot an accusatory glance at his wife, who cried, "Don't blame me! Don't you dare blame this one on me!"

Beside her, Chappie spoke up suddenly. "Wait, do you *know* them? Do you know the Johnsons? It's a small world."

"No, I don't know them," Frances said.

"You know the Johnsons?" This was Tommy again. "How do you like that? Jeez, what are the chances?"

"No, I don't! I don't know them—"

"Well, let me be clear—I want to be perfectly clear!" A respectful hush came over the table as the host drew himself up. He spoke in a measured, serious tone, full of consideration. "It had nothing to do with the fact that Rich Johnson is Black and his wife is the…you know, the whatchamacallit. Nothing to do with it at all. Ask anyone around this table. Anyone at all. I wasn't born with a silver spoon in my mouth—I'm friends with all kinds of people, all kinds. Guy I work with, he's Black. He's been with us since we started. Great guy! Superior guy. One of the best. He and I get lunch first Thursday of every month. Ask anyone! Ask anyone here! Isn't Nattie-O my best pal—Annie! Hey! Annie!"

"Don't say *Black*, Chappie, dear—it's *African-American!*"

Pam and Theresa and Annie shook with silent mirth.

"I have never understood this," Pilar remarked. "Why they call themselves African-American. Are they from Africa or America? It is necessary to choose, no?"

"NWA in the actual White House, I'm telling you!" TZ stretched lazily and yawned. "All bets are off!" He rose to his feet and began to dance in place at the head of the table, swiveling his hips and using the wine bottle as a microphone.

"He's gonna do it!" Pam clapped her hands together.

"'Straight outta Compton, crazy motherfucker—'"

"TZ!" screamed Annie in delight. She balled up a napkin and threw it at him.

Felipe caught Frances's eye flirtatiously. "Well, then, *I* am also offended! My wife is from Madrid, Frances, and I am offended that you do not refer to her as European-American! Do you hear me? I am offended!"

"'Crazy motherfucker named Ice Cube!!' Something, something, something, something, *some*thing..."

"Well, then, how about *colored?*" Chappie snapped. "Can I say *colored?* How about that? Or how about *Negro?* Does that work for you? Or what about just plain old fucking—"

Frances's hands jerked. Her wineglass smashed to the floor.

For a moment, the room was absolutely silent. Then they all burst into astonished laughter and applause. "And on her first night!" Pam cried over the hooting and the clapping. "Her very first night!"

From the foot of the table, Annie raised her glass to the newcomer. "Well, hallelujah! You're christened now, Frances!" she cried. "You're one of us!"

Nude Hose

In Mead, Massachusetts, the town where Susanna Gutteridge grew up, there was a boarding school, also called Mead. A few of the town kids went to Mead Hall every year as day students, but Susanna was not among them. Her parents'—Eddy and Cynthia's—relationship with the school was a static one. They were glad in some mild, unarticulated way that the school was in their town because they were town-proud, and the school had a national reputation, but beyond that, it was distinct from their lives, apart from their knowing the head of athletics, the school nurse, Mrs. Olson, and those few teachers who made a point of getting to know the townspeople—Señor Villegas, for instance, who lunched with the Rotary Club at Hannafin's on Wednesdays.

Susanna was a bright, biddable child, watchful, and occasionally afraid. As a little girl, she was afraid more often than either of her parents had expected his or her offspring to be. Because of this slight timidity, Cynthia wanted to consider homeschooling their daughter. Eddy was against it, though. A compact man with an explosive energy, Eddy Gutteridge had been a three-sport athlete in high school. Of below-average height, he had the advantage of speed. He objected to his wife's plans infrequently, rarely seeing the need. But the summer Susanna turned five years old, they fought about it, evenings after they'd eaten supper out on the screened porch.

"She's an only child, for God's sake! She's gotta get out, Cynnie! She's gotta make friends!"

Night after night, Eddy's argument was met with silence. Cynthia would sit calmly with her hands folded in her lap, looking through the porch screen to the line of fir trees where their yard ended. Through the trees you could glimpse their neighbors' backyard—the bright blue of a tarp that covered their woodpile. After a couple of minutes, Cynthia would get up to clear. She would stand over the garbage in the kitchen and dump the gnawed corncobs into the plastic pail, then peel off the white paper plates from the round wicker baskets and throw them in too. Eddy didn't bend, and that September Cynthia relinquished Susanna to kindergarten in the Mead school system.

The high school, referred to as "Regional," combined students from Mead and Minnechaug, the next town over—the bigger town, with the traffic circle and the Wendy's. The teenage Susanna Gutteridge raced through Regional as if she were gunning a car on a downhill, piling on extra-credit classes and APs and optional assignments with an alacrity that struck some of her peers as masochistic. Academically, she had proven to

be ambidextrous—as good at biology and math as she was at
English essays and *explications de texte*. Her report cards, straight
As semester after semester, might have come to seem to her
teachers more like administrative forms to be filled out than
real honors duly earned.

She cheated once on a test. It was a makeup for a quiz
on *Huckleberry Finn* that she'd missed because of a rare sick
day. Sabotaged, she'd been—bleeding through pads at such an
alarming rate, she was afraid to go to school and unwilling
to have another anxious, angry-making session in the upstairs
bathroom to try to get a tampon up there. With any other
student in the school, the AP English teacher Mr. Frye would
have supervised the makeup in person, but he allowed Susanna
Gutteridge to take it alone in one of the lightly graffitied carrels
at the back of the library (*Chem sux ass; Regional girls luv cock*,
graphic included, in the moment of orgasm) while he taught
his tenth-grade class on *Macbeth*.

Susanna was the kind of girl who rereads *Pride and Prejudice*
every six months, who discovers Wilkie Collins on her own.
She found Twain hokey and irritating, and she had done something that spring that surprised even her: she had refused to
really read the book, skimming it disdainfully instead, holding
it literally at arm's length to get through the assignments, as if
the prose might somehow seep into her skin and infect her. She
had missed the part about the duke and the king entirely. She
had no idea who they were, so when she got a question about
them on the makeup quiz, she leaned down and withdrew the
black and green paperback from her backpack on the floor. She
thumbed through it till she found the chapter, keeping an eye
on the librarian, Mrs. Kovalcek, who was notating card-catalog

cards at her desk. As Susanna ran her eyes down the pages that contained the relevant episode, she got absorbed momentarily in the story of the two hustlers who make Huck and Jim do their bidding. When Huck and Jim agreed to call those condescending assholes "Your Lordship" and "Your Majesty," she could have thrown the book across the room, she was so mad. A sound of disgust escaped her throat and she had to pretend to have a coughing fit so that Mrs. Kovalcek wouldn't suspect anything. As soon as she had the opportunity, she pushed the book back down into her backpack. "How *could* they?" she kept saying to herself, meaning Huck and Jim. How could they just roll over like that and take it? Let these self-styled aristocrats but actually fucking assholes the duke and the king walk all over them—and then say it was easy, as if it cost them nothing?

"Since we all know who's the valedictorian," Mr. Deluca, the principal, opened Regional's commencement that year, "and we have known it for months…no, forget it, for years, maybe ever since Cynthia Gutteridge came home from Minnechaug Memorial Hospital eighteen years ago"—he paused to guffaw—"may I suggest that you all focus on the salutatorian race, where at least there's still some suspense!"

Susanna won so many National Merit awards, scholarship grants, state honors, and the like, Sandy Ripley joked with Eddy and Cynthia after the ceremony that they were going to be able to pay for their retirement with all the cash she was raking in.

"You're onto us!" Eddy barked. "Soon's she's out the door, Cyn and I are heading to Florida! Got a nice little condo all picked out!"

Cynthia thanked Sandy with an air of forbearance. Susanna's mother had had her beatific look on all morning. It was as if she were privy to some trumping knowledge that would soon render pointless the petty preoccupations of this warm June graduation day—its hackneyed celebration and predictably ensuing emotions. The expression closed her off from the other joking giddy mothers—and that suited Cynthia just fine. She had no interest in joining in, as Eddy did with the dads, the group congratulations. At Hannafin's afterward, Cynthia sat slightly apart from the crowd of parents and graduates eating ice cream at the outdoor picnic tables. She mentally repudiated the false modesty of her husband's cooperative banter—"D'ja ever think we'd get 'em this far?" "You're telling me!" She hated the way Eddy went along with it, pretending that Susanna was like any Mead schoolchild when they both knew she was nothing like the rest of them. Nothing like them at all. Susanna was different. Susanna was special. Susanna had turned out to be very bright—brighter even than Cynthia had hoped.

Susanna worked that summer, as she had for the past two, for Mr. Ripley in his landscaping business. Eddy had gotten her the job originally. It paid the best of any of the jobs in Mead open to high-school students—better than lifeguarding at the pond or babysitting. Susanna rode shotgun in the pickup truck with Andy Devlin, a young guy from town; she supervised the three junior-high-school boys who mowed the lawns with push mowers and weeded the beds while she or Andy weed-whacked or handled the pruning together or, as of the middle of July, sneaked back to the truck to fool around.

On the Friday of the week the fooling around had started,

33

the two of them stood talking after work in the parking lot of Ripley's, which was just a lot by the side of Route 11 on the way out of town. Mr. Ripley had his office in a detached trailer beside a large gray metal warehouse where the landscaping equipment was stored; there was a dump of gravel out back.

"Give you a ride home?" Andy asked her, throwing down his cigarette.

Technically, only certain designated vehicles were allowed onto the Beale Sanctuary. The grounds of the two-hundred-acre former estate were preserved for walking and horseback riding; cross-country skiing in winter. Andy drove way in off the street, bumping along the deeply rutted dirt road for three-quarters of a mile. The Datsun's transmission kept scraping the ground where the ridge in the middle of the road was the highest. He parked in a copse of pines beside Drear Pond and had sex with her, starting out in the hot, stale-smelling car and finishing up on the ground, root-riddled and blanketed with pine needles. She didn't tell him she was a virgin, and if he noticed, he didn't say anything.

Afterward, when she was sitting up and drawing her clothes to her in what she hoped was a nonchalant manner, Andy said, "Now that we've had sex, will you marry me, Susanna?"

"Right," Susanna said. "Uh-huh."

"The fuck? I'm serious!"

Susanna ignored him and concentrated on getting dressed, getting her underpants over her ankles and up her legs, feeling around for her bra. She knew how crazy the boy could get. When they were working, Andy never missed an opportunity to pretend the hose was his dick as he sprayed the flower beds or to pantomime jerking off if one of the homeowners came out and reprimanded the crew about the music on their boom box being too loud. All boys pantomimed jerking off, of course, but with the boys in her class, Susanna had always felt they were making gestures and foul noises to humiliate her. She assumed, as she had since fourth or fifth grade, that she was the butt of their jokes, and she would pretend not to notice. But Andy's behavior had an inclusivity to it. It was actually funny, watching him pretend the hose was his dick spraying the flower beds.

"I'm totally serious," he repeated.

"Uh-huh, sure you are." Susanna held up her Ripley's T-shirt and shook the pine needles off of it.

She could feel Andy's shrewd eyes on her, assessing her. She couldn't find the bra so she was just going to put the T-shirt on without it, but then she felt the metal closure under her thigh. She pulled it out and turned it over so it was right-side out. He was still watching her.

She swallowed. "What the hell, Andy?"

"Susanna!" He pinned her wrists together so fast that she didn't have time to be afraid. Her hands were still holding the bra, only helplessly now, the satin and wire crushed between them. "I'm asking you a *question*. Will you or won't you, Susanna? Susanna Gutteridge. Susanna from the *gutter. Ridge.* Answer. The question. Answer it!"

"Okay!" Susanna gave an uptight little laugh. "I heard you!" She desperately needed to swallow again but she didn't want to give herself away as being nervous—pathetic. Her breasts were hanging down—a feeling she loathed because it made her feel untidy. She even slept in a bra, one of those pajama ones with no underwire.

35

"Answer the question, Gutteridge. Will you marry me?"

There was no twinkle in his eye to let her off the hook, to indicate the marriage proposal was a joke. Well, that was Andy Devlin for you. He always took it to the max. A touch of suspicion in his eyes, as if deep down he doubted her—thought she was a fraud—was his only discernible expression. She could see the dots in his skin—the dozens of minuscule holes across his cheeks and nose that he'd gotten from smoking.

"That's right, Andy. Ri-i-i-ight." Her voice cracked. She sounded like an idiot. She sounded like a fraud. "I'm going to marry you. I'm going to marry you and just bail on college and my parents and everything."

Feeling foolish, she made herself keep looking into his eyes. Andy held the deadened, forbidding expression for a second. Then he laughed and released her wrists. She got her bra hooked around her waist, even with her clumsy and slow fingers.

"Look at these fucking tits!" he murmured. He got up on his knees, totally naked, cupped his hands around his mouth, and hollered into the woods, "These are some incredible fucking tits we got here!"

"Shh! Shh!" Susanna didn't know whether to laugh or to cry. "Andy, stop! People will hear!" As quickly as she could, she pulled up the bra straps, yanked her T-shirt over her head.

Still kneeling, Andy picked up a stone and threw it expertly at the surface of the pond; it skipped half a dozen times.

"Impressive." When Susanna had her shorts on and was shimmying them over her hips, he leaned over and gripped her thigh between his thumb and fingers. "Look at that thigh."

"Ow!" Susanna said and then, plaintively, "Andy!" It didn't

really hurt, but predictable girlie expressions were her new specialty; it was as if she'd been learning and internalizing them all these years like some pathetically conscientious understudy.

"You're that runner chick." Andy nodded, narrowing his eyes. "I seen you."

That he had just used the past participle incorrectly was more startling to her in its way than the marriage proposal of a moment ago, but Susanna didn't react outwardly.

She had spent a lot of time preparing for the future these four years—going on diets with Cynthia, putting her photographs in albums, sorting all her old clothes into piles to give away—but when you got involved in something, she realized all at once, your preparations were for naught. Whatever it was you got into, it just flowed over you.

"What if I left you here and you had to hike out?" Andy said when he was back in his jeans and she was dressed and on her feet, dusting the debris of the forest floor off her thighs. He was leaning against the car, lighting one of the Marlboro Reds he smoked incessantly. His voice was so harsh, it stopped her cold. She simply couldn't think of an answer. Then he laughed again.

"Naw, I'm just kidding. Get in—I'll take you home."

"I intimidate them!"

"You intimidate them!"

"We both intimidate them!"

That was the theory on which Susanna and her friend Stacey Larsen had relied over the years regarding the boys at Regional. For her part, Susanna was half right. She did intimidate them, not simply with her straight As but with her haughty carriage—uncompromising in spite of her height and the big, generous shelf of a chest that would have stooped another girl's shoulders. Hers was certainly not a runner's body, but Susanna Gutteridge had not let that stop her.

The boys would see her starting her run at the swampy bottom of Route 11 where it met Long Meadow Road when they were on their way to town to buy candy and doughnuts and cigarettes at New England Pantry, Brian Berry driving the Mazda, his fat knees poking out on either side of the steering wheel, AC/DC blaring on the radio. When they had scoped the fridge for beers that Brian's brother Dennis would buy them Friday night (sixes of Coors or Miller Genuine Draft or Rolling Rock in bottles), they would head home, maybe a quarter of an hour later, their restlessness deferred—tamped down, merely. And there she would be, grinding over the insulting last rise of that relentless hill, her face set in its typically obtuse squint, as if she were straining to look farther ahead of her than her contact-lens prescription allowed. The girl's self-punishing dedication to jogging imposed a jittery silence on them as they drove by. None of the boys would call to her, but none of them jeered at her either. They paid Susanna Gutteridge the sort of respect you might pay a house of worship not your own—finding yourself inside it, understanding the quiet, the gravity owed, not cowed so much as discomfited by a sudden acute awareness of the irrelevance of your presence.

In social studies once—it must have been junior spring—during a rowdy debate on secessionism, Susanna had seized Brian Berry's forearm (a brief grasp in which one of her long unpainted nails marked the soft skin on the underside of his arm before, without looking at him, she let it go). He had been surprised at the readiness with which his groin stirred, as if he'd secretly been hot for Gutteridge all these years. He'd dreamed about her after that, about tit-fucking those 36-double-Ds, and when people complained about her—though she was the topic of conversation less often than she imagined—he'd say with a mixture of exasperation and dismay, "She just needs to get laid!"

Susanna went from not knowing how to kiss—her back against the forest-green Ripley pickup truck, parked in broad daylight on Dale Street outside the yellow house and barn they did on Tuesdays, her lips pressed shut until, with a shock of enlightenment, she felt his tongue probing her teeth and belatedly opened her mouth—to going all the way with Andy every Friday afternoon in the Beale Sanctuary. She counted down the weeks till she was to leave for the small liberal arts college in western Massachusetts whose campus, she recalled frequently and with satisfaction—often during the act of sex itself—was neat and bucolic and somehow, unlike the Ivies she might have shot for, within her ken: it was how she had pictured college. The neoclassical buildings, the ancient elms and maples, the students lying half on top of one another in clusters on a lush green lawn.

Only the summer before, Andy Devlin had seemed oafish and irrelevant—improbably tall, with gangling apelike arms. He looked a bit like an ape: the overlong torso, hunched to mask his height, his eyes a little too close together in what Susanna recalled Stacey's mother, who was nosy and interfering, calling a "mongoloid" sort of way. Or maybe it was simply logistics that had kept her from noticing him. Last summer Andy had worked only one day a week for Ripley's. He was trying out a grounds-crew job over at Mead Hall—not Mead-Minnechaug Regional High School, where Susanna went, but the boarding school that was on the other side of town. Something was off about his dismissal; Susanna wasn't sure how she knew that—if, indeed, she actually knew that—or even whether he'd quit or been fired from the job. Despite his reputation for impatience and terseness, Eddy was a big gossip. He knew everything going on in town. In July, when she and Andy had started hooking up, Susanna tried to remember: What was it her dad had said offhandedly to Cynthia the previous summer? That night when the two of them were sitting out on the screen porch discussing Andy's having been let go—before Susanna had cared enough to pay attention? *Ben Devlin's kid got himself into trouble again over at Mead Hall,* Eddy had said. And then keeping himself well apart when her mother had expressed sympathy. *Big risk they were taking, when you think about it.*

"Wasn't for me that job," Susanna had heard Andy tell Mrs. Ripley the other day when she came by to drop off Sandy's sub for lunch. "I'm glad-a be back." He had a slow, slack way of talking, a drawl almost, and the spit collected in his mouth, giving his speech an attractive slur. His thick hair was not truly blond but also not brown or light brown. It was cut shorter on top and longer in the back, and his skin was being ruined from smoking. He was twenty-three years old.

"You shouldn't smoke, you know," Susanna told him one Friday afternoon in August when Andy was driving her home.

Andy didn't smoke casually, as the high-school boys—Brian Berry and the rest—tried to, effeminate hands on American

40

Spirits that they stabbed out after a few drags, though he smoked constantly. Andy consumed the cigarette; he possessed it; he *was* it. He could do anything with a cigarette—he could talk while he smoked, he could weed-whack two-handed; his exhales could be comic or tragic; there were a dozen things he could do with his fingers and a book of matches.

He slowed the car at the Yield sign where 11 ran into Old Minnechaug Road and made a magician-like flourish as he withdrew a second cigarette from behind his ear and lit it with the first. "Fuckin' A!" he hollered out the car window, grinning his toothy grin.

"You could get cancer, you know!" Susanna persisted, raising her voice over the Datsun's transmission. "Or emphysema!"

They were leaving the bucolic side of Mead, with the trim nineteenth-century colonials in white, gray, and yellow, all with black shutters, and the long quiet stone walls fencing the large contiguous fields that were still hayed. Mead Hall, the boarding school, was behind them and the town was before them and beyond the town came the newer houses.

A lot of the lawns Ripley's Landscaping was responsible for belonged to the houses that had been put up on the far side of town, the recently developed side of Mead. In this part of town, there had been no long-term cultivation. The pines were simply cleared, the pastel houses built, the postholes dug for the mailboxes that, along with the swing sets and patios with barbecues out back, meant *People live here now.*

Neither the Gutteridges' house nor the Devlins' house was so easily delineated. Susanna's house was an upright Victorian on Pleasant Street, a block from the post office, in a row of upright Victorians, the house her mother had grown up in back when she was Cynthia Boylan. Andy lived with his parents in a long shutterless farmhouse on the border of Minnechaug. At the end of the Devlins' driveway, there was a faded wooden sign in the shape of a poodle sitting up to beg with the words—always so intriguing to Susanna—LICENSED DOG FANCIER. Mrs. Devlin ran a dog-grooming business out of her house and raised puppies, the ones Susanna thought of as miniature collies but that were actually, she had now learned from Andy, called shelties.

His fingers on the bottom of the wheel, Andy turned his head and kept his eyes on her for a disconcertingly long time. "Andy! The road!" she screamed as the car veered off it onto the grassy verge. He shifted into second and took the sedan back onto the blacktop as an irate horn sounded behind them.

"Jesus Christ, Andy!"

"Emphysema, huh?" He took a drag on the cigarette. "How do you know all these diseases?"

"What? Are you kidding? Everybody knows about emphysema." He was going into the probing, prosecutorial mode that always irritated her and that, this last week or so, in the relentless August humidity, had started to drive her crazy. "Come on, didn't you have the Cigarette Guy, the Anti-Smoking Guy come to your class? We used to flush my mom's down the toilet." Susanna cackled at the memory of herself and her dad ganging up on Cynthia—for her own good, of course.

After a minute during which he drove and smoked with a preoccupied look on his face, Andy said, "Are your parents doctors?"

Susanna expelled air through her nose. "No, Andy."

"They're not?"

"No! They're not fucking doctors! What the hell?"

"They're not lawyers, are they?"

"No!" she wailed. "You know my dad—Eddy! Boylan and Wells! Come on! Don't you have our oil?"

"Oh, yeah, duh…Boylan and Wells. I knew that. Well, what about your mother? What about Cynthia Boylan Gutteridge?"

"Oh, you know." The topic of her mother bored and irritated Susanna. She looked out the window as they passed the old graveyard where, in elementary school, she and Stacey Larsen had played among the friendly, lichen-covered headstones—not hide-and-seek, though sometimes there were other kids there who played that or capture the flag. She and Stacey had pretended they lived in the cemetery, and the headstones were their houses, their school, their churches—Stacey was Unitarian and Susanna was a Christmas-and-Easter Episcopalian, so there were always two churches in the game.

"She teaches art."

"At the high school?"

"No, at Tech."

"In Minnechaug?"

Susanna nodded. "Art and, like, ceramics. Shit like that."

"Did she teach Marge?" Marge was Andy's older sister—long gone; married, now, in Maine. "She went to Tech."

Her mind wandering, Susanna said nothing.

Andy glanced at her and said sharply, "Hey! I'm not making this up," as if she had contradicted him.

"Fine, Andy! I never said—"

"I should have gone to Tech instead of friggin' Regional! Maybe then I would have finished. G.E.D.s suck ass."

"Yeah, well…"

Andy smoked and brooded till they were nearly at her house. "So, do you *know* any lawyers?"

"No." Susanna was so exasperated she could have cried. Then something came to her. "Wait, you know what? Joey's mom is a lawyer. She has that sign out, right? In front of her house? 'Attorney-at-law.'"

"Yeah?"

"Why?" Susanna said suspiciously. "You need a lawyer?"

He didn't respond to the sarcasm in her voice, didn't seem, particularly, to register it. He exhaled slowly without bothering to turn his head to the window as he usually did. Susanna coughed and batted the smoke away.

"I'm trying to get my case heard," he said. "These people— they're trying to lock me up."

"Uh-huh."

"I'm serious! I am one hundred percent totally fucking serious."

"Okay, Andy. Whatever you say."

"They try to control me with medication, see. They don't want me to be my real self. That scares them—the truth scares them. That's why I need to get a lawyer." He looked at her. After a second, he grinned. "Naw, I'm just kidding."

The senior class from Regional had come explosively together, sanctioned by the complete breaking down of barriers that followed graduation. Susanna knew all about it because now even Stacey Larsen was going to parties. The past Saturday, she confessed to Susanna on the phone, she had let Dennis Berry put his hands down her pants behind the Donnellys' barn. She had given him a blow job. Or thought she had. She wasn't sure it counted, she was gagging so bad.

Susanna was busy too, her last summer at home. She had cajoled Eddy into training with her for the Rotary Club 10K race. She'd had to get after him when, in the event, he quit after 5K and ducked into Hannafin's for coffee with the boys. On Tuesday nights, she went with Cynthia to a series of classical brass concerts at St. Andrew's, the Episcopal church in Minnechaug. And Sundays she had breakfast with Eddy at Hannafin's. They always sat at the counter on the faded green vinyl swivel stools. Lynn the waitress would josh Susanna's dad. She'd slap him with the plastic menu. Eddy was popular in town, unlike his wife, who was considered a troublemaker— the kind of person who tried to ban the Dunkin' Donuts they wanted to put in at the Mobil station and backed candidates trying to defeat Arnie Towle, the district's longtime Republican congressman. Somehow Eddy managed to keep apart from all that, from causes; people in the town didn't necessarily associate him with his wife. After she brought Eddy's coffee, Lynn would jerk a thumb toward Susanna. "You must be prouda this one! Valedictorian, eh? Not too fucking bad! Oops—'scuse my French, Eddy."

Susanna and Cynthia made trifle, as they always did, for Eddy's birthday on August 17. Cynthia picked Susanna up at Ripley's after work and they drove to Castellucci's for ladyfingers and jam. The old pharmacy next to the grocery store sold the kind of stockings they both liked—nude, sandal-foot, and (the tricky thing to find) *not* control-top, which neither of them liked. On their way in, they ran into Mrs. Devlin coming out. You never saw Mr. Devlin in town. Ben Devlin had had a stroke years ago and was in a wheelchair. But it wasn't unusual for Cynthia and Susanna, doing errands like this, to run into Patty. You knew her, as you knew most people in Mead, by her car—the rust-colored pickup with the hard plastic top over the truck bed and the wide white stripe down the side. There were always two or three dogs in the front seat and a sign taped to the back window that said AKC-REGISTERED PUPPIES.

Cynthia spoke kindly to Mrs. Devlin. "How's Ben doing, Patty? How are you getting on?" With people like Mrs. Devlin, Cynthia was always kind, never pretentious.

"'Bout the same, to be honest!" Patty said, and she laughed, embarrassed. Patty Devlin was always laughing, always embarrassed. Susanna was praying she'd get by without a mention of Andy when Mrs. Devlin looked right at her and said, "You and Andy are having some fun, huh?"

Susanna felt her stomach contract, but Mrs. Devlin's expression was guileless, the embarrassment gone—concern, in fact, in its place, but a calm, professional concern, a bit like she'd looked when a dog got hit by a car outside the post office and Susanna and Eddy, going in to get their mail, had seen her surveying the animal to see if it could be helped.

"Oh, yes, we are!" Susanna said. "And the other kids— the younger kids—they've really gotten so much better. It's a great job!" she added for the benefit of her mother. She looked cautiously at Mrs. Devlin and then saw it all at once—that with Patty Devlin, it was all right; that at the Devlins', it was all out in the open. Not the fucking, of course. But she sensed, from Mrs. Devlin's manner, that in Andy's house, he and she might be an item. That floored her for a second, picturing herself as a member of the kind of family where she'd announce casually, *Yeah, Andy Devlin and I are seeing each other. It's pretty fun.*

The dogs' barking from across the parking lot was growing frenzied. "They see Mom, they go crazy," Mrs. Devlin said apologetically, the embarrassment back.

"You say hi to Ben for me," Cynthia said.

"Oh, I always do. You're one of the ones he remembers!"

"We were Town Pond lifeguards together!" Cynthia said, as she always did.

"Bye, Mrs. Devlin!" Susanna said.

"You take care of yourself, Susanna," Andy's mother said, holding her gaze.

Susanna glossed over the solemnity in the woman's voice by laughing and saying, "Oh, I will! I always do!" as if Mrs. Devlin had used the expression the way most adults did, as just another way of saying goodbye.

Then it was the next-to-last Friday in August. The following week, Susanna would work for Mr. Ripley on Monday and Tuesday only. On Wednesday she had to finish packing. On Thursday, they'd be on 495 South to the Mass Pike, to college.

"You know, I went to your house once when I was little," Susanna told Andy that afternoon in the Beale Sanctuary. "My babysitter was friends with Marge."

She had been sitting, dressed and ready to go, with her back up against a pine tree for half an hour. She killed mosquitoes against her arms and thighs, trying not to act fed up, and watched Andy as he smoked, moody and still naked, and paced along the bank of the river.

Andy had gotten bored with their spot by the pond. Today he had driven right past the familiar pine trees and deeper into the woods to where the grassy road forked at a stone stile, the left-veering branch going quickly downhill to the Nassatog River, on the far side of which lay the Georgian brick buildings of Mead Hall.

The Mead Hall crews practiced on the Nassatog. Two or three times, on exercise walks she took with Cynthia, Susanna had seen the students appear in their long, slim boats, barely visible as they cleaved the river before them and came into view, the oars of the shells moving in systematized effort, followed by a motorboat that zipped back and forth making profligate arcs in the water. When she was with Cynthia, she had prayed the rowers wouldn't notice them up on the bank, and the rowers never did, consumed as they were by the task at hand. Once, though, a kid riding in the motorboat had raised a blank, insolent face to her, and she had almost waved before, in the nick of time, she'd stilled her hand. It was the same when she was with Eddy at Hannafin's and a group of Mead boys came in and took the big table at the back. She had the same sense that they had seen her and not seen her. If she liked her outfit on a particular day, she would hope to be noticed. If she didn't, she would hope to pass invisibly. But she had never wished for invisibility more than she did today, with Andy—despite the fact that her anxiety was ridiculous. It was summer. Mead Hall was not in session. The water was calm and flat. The boats would not appear, and no one would ever see her there.

"Did you hear me?" she persisted. "Marge knew my baby-sitter, so I went to your house. She took me up to see the dogs one time."

"Who was your babysitter?" Andy hurled his cigarette into the river.

"Kim Carson?"

"That slut."

Susanna giggled, but Andy didn't echo it. He turned and came up the bank toward her. He was in a bad mood today. There was something in his eyes—not anger but an angry wariness, as if he knew he was being double-crossed but hadn't figured out who the traitor was. She'd heard Mr. Ripley chewing him out about something this morning when Eddy dropped her off, really lighting into him, but not like a boss, like an exasperated parent. *Come on, Andy—I'm giving you a chance here!*

They'd already had sex once, but he'd been frantic to come again, groaning in outrage when it didn't work. He was standing in front of her now, his thing—everything—in her face.

"You know what? Give me a blow job."

Susanna gave a scornful laugh and turned her head away, toward the river. "Yeah, right."

"Hey!" He snapped his fingers. "Come on!"

She put a hand to her eyes to block the late-afternoon sun and tilted her head up to him. "Uh-huh. Right, Andy. In your dreams."

"What the fuck?" He seized her shoulders and shoved his penis toward her.

"Eww! Jesus!" She recoiled, covering her face.

"Hurry up! I mean it."

"This is such a fucking joke, Andy!" she said. "I want to go home. I'm tired! Can you just take me home? I mean—for God's sake!"

"Guess you'll have to walk, then."

Susanna folded her arms across her chest and waited. A number of thoughts passed through her head slowly, disconnectedly. She looked out at the river and wondered whether her college roommate, whose name and address in Tokyo she'd just been given, would invite her to Japan next summer. She hoped so. She really wanted to see the Far East.

They argued about it some more. Susanna tried to jolly him out of it. Ripley's was hard physical work, and despite the humidity, she could feel herself growing cold, sitting on the ground, in the clammy way you did when your sweat dried on you. She was supposed to watch a movie with Cynthia tonight—a black-and-white one; she couldn't remember the name, but Cynthia said she knew she'd love it. With Bette Davis, maybe. A few stray storm clouds partially covered the setting sun. But eventually, she just gave in.

He sat down in the driver's side of the car, the door open, and she got on her knees on the ground in front of him and she did it. It took forever. It was so tedious, so tiresome and disgusting, she could have screamed. At last she remembered something Stacey Larsen had told her. You were supposed to make a ring of your thumb and index finger and move it up and down over the head of the guy's thing. "They'll come right away, I swear to God." It worked and Andy grunted in relief. He had a six-pack of orange soda in the back seat and on the way home, he gave her one to get the taste out of her mouth. He made some funny deprecating comments about himself. "Nice, Devlin. Real nice."

On Sunday at Hannafin's, Lynn brought Eddy's coffee out to him, and they had a chuckle over the latest news—the now twice-widowed Carlene Munson had taken up with John Tartaglia when, as Eddy put it, "Roger was still warm!"

When the waitress went back into the kitchen, Eddy ripped the tops off two sugars, poured them into his coffee, and stirred—a series of gestures, Susanna realized, she had seen him make a thousand times. "Good thing you're nearly done at Ripley's," Eddy said, slowly stirring. "What do you got? Two more days?"

"Yeah," Susanna said peaceably, "I'm ready to be done."

"You'll be on your own. I ran into Connie Ripley at the post office." Eddy took the spoon out of the mug and laid it on the counter. "Andy Devlin got hauled off to Memorial last night." He paused. "Second time in six months."

Susanna was aware of her father's face without actually looking at it as, eyes bright over the mug, he took a slow sip of his coffee. She was aware of his tone too, the satisfied chuckle with which he delivered all of the town's gossip but particularly the kind that caught someone out—exposed an affair or some smaller failing, a drunken embarrassment, a public fight. She noticed the way, just a little too quickly, he added the detail about its being the "second time in six months." He added it the way you rush to relate all the details of a victory—that you not only beat someone but beat them by a decisive margin, trounced them to bits.

"Got hauled off in a straitjacket."

"Did he?" Susanna took a napkin from the dispenser on the counter and held it to her lap, closing her hand around it. "God—poor Andy." She cleared her throat and wiped at a spot on the counter. "That sucks."

"Put up quite a fight, evidently."

"Wow." There wasn't the slightest tremble in her voice, but now Susanna did look at Eddy. She looked straight at his profile, but he didn't turn to meet her eyes. He brought the mug up carefully to his lips again, his gaze going to the kitchen door as it swung open and first the younger, newer waitress and then Lynn hustled out, their arms laden with plates.

"They got him in it eventually, I guess, and they hauled him right off."

"Well, that's good, at least."

"Who knows how long he'll be locked up."

"Yeah, well," Susanna said, "what can you do?"

Eddy, she knew, was expecting her to be shocked. He was perhaps expecting her to say *You're kidding me!* or maybe *What? My God—I had no idea!* She said neither of these things. Lying in her bed weeks ago, she had remembered the story about Andy's getting fired from the Mead Hall job the summer before. The specific circumstances of his being let go didn't come back to her, but the conversation her parents had had about it, which she'd overheard, did. She had been able to recall Eddy's comment all along, that there was something "off" about the way he left. That he had "got himself into trouble again over at Mead Hall." But a few weeks ago, Susanna had remembered Cynthia's reply. She repeated it now: "Schizophrenia is a terrible disease," she said.

"Got that right!" Eddy was busy with his utensils, straightening them on the paper place mat.

"Here's your syrup, honey." Lynn put down the Mrs. Butterworth's on the counter. This was one of the many reasons Cynthia refused to dine at Hannafin's: they didn't serve real maple syrup.

"Thanks, Lynn," said Susanna, "thanks so much," and she poured the fake stuff over her waffles.

It proved handy, freshman year, to have Andy Devlin up her sleeve. The story could be played many ways, depending on the audience and the desired effect: "My boyfriend back home," or simply "The guy I lost it to," or, when she wanted to sound experienced and blasé, "This crazy guy I dated. No— I mean *literally* crazy!" The few times Susanna actually went into details—"He got hauled off in a straitjacket…can you imagine?"—she could sense the power she had over her audience, though to her the Andy story was as tired and clichéd as the English papers poor students like Brian Berry had written, which she and Stacey Larsen used to write parodies of: "The author is trying to get across the point that love is the only thing in life that matters even when somebody is being convinced by another person that their [*sic*] alone in the universe…"

One early-autumn afternoon at the beginning of a long first semester filled with false starts, she attended a meeting at the college's women's center—an attempt at finding herself so misguided it could still make her wince twenty years later. The young women sat in folding chairs placed in a circle, and the student leader encouraged them all to share with the others any time they had felt afraid (the implication being "at the hands of a man"). Offering up the story on cue—her instinct for the A still sharp as ever—Susanna tried to conjure a feeling of victimization to match the narrative: the time he had kept her there by the Nassatog, down on her knees in the most humiliating position, doing the most humiliating act…But she couldn't work up much angst about it, try as she might. She felt more traumatized by the moment when she looked around, mid-sharing, and noticed that while she was wearing nylons, all of the other young women's legs were bare, and many of them not only bare but unshaven. She was the only one who had pantyhose on. That mistake—that took her years to get over. As well as a comment on her naïveté—the goody-two-shoes mindset she'd cultivated, thinking it would protect her—it seemed to have class implications. She fled the women's center the moment the meeting ended and never returned. She got onto the social-activities committee instead.

But Andy Devlin didn't keep her up nights. She understood something now. Her AP English teacher, Mr. Frye, would have been proud of her, if only she could have told him.

That line from *Huck Finn* (which she'd gone back and read, almost in spite of herself, in late-night chunks over her last summer at home) repeated itself in her head that whole first year of college, that part she hadn't known for the test, when the king and the duke take up residence on the raft, and they make Huck and Jim start calling them "Your Highness" and "Your Lordship," and Huck says, "That was easy, so we done it."

That was all easy, so we done it.

A Blind Corner

They could go in not speaking a word of Italian and come out fluent! They could practically *be* Italian," Alison Spalding said to her husband. It was a fine July evening in Tuscany. She and Tim were sitting outside at the restaurant across the bridge from the *agriturismo* where they were staying. Crowded with tourists, the restaurant's terrace was hard on the road, but the road itself was mainly quiet. When a car did appear, it whizzed into sight, then had to slow down as it passed in order to make the hairpin turn by the church down the way. The Tuscans drove like maniacs but in cars that were so small, the speed had a comic effect—they looked like insects, Alison thought as she watched a blue Fiat disappear, or game pieces. The air was dry and sweet, redolent of wild mint. In the field across the road from Il Girasole, the thousands of sunflowers from which the place took its name stood at attention, all facing west toward the setting sun.

"Almost gives me the creeps, how they stand like that," Alison had observed when they sat down.

"Fascist flowers," Tim joked, following her gaze. "Like a remnant from the country's past." Early on, when they were still only dating, he had perceived that a current of irony might help temper Alison's earnest, emotional interface with the world.

"We could put them in a real Italian school!" she persisted, with some urgency, though it was a theoretical "them" she referred to. She was not yet pregnant. Married a year, they were waiting one more year to have children for no real reason other than the vague, generationally endorsed one of taking one's last unencumbered trips abroad.

In the decade after college, Alison had worked at two or three different jobs—advertising, on the creative side; an aggregate art-sales website whose founder she knew socially— but never settled in one long enough to call it a career. More than once, at the moment when she would have had to double down—work the hours, put up with the unreasonable boss— her commitment had foundered on what seemed to her a moral issue. "I would have had to compromise everything I believe in!" she would explain. Nicely educated with a degree from a liberal arts college and exuding an air of curiosity as well as responsibility, she made do between full-time jobs tutoring high-school students in essay writing, house-sitting, dog-sitting, watering plants. Then, toward the end of the '90s, when those kinds of gigs had begun to appear less readily and she felt as if people were starting to be embarrassed to ask her, she met Tim. He was fresh out of law school, starting in litigation at one of the big firms.

"A *local* school, I mean." She gave a critical look around the terrace as a table of Germans exploded into laughter. "Not one of those international warehouses for expats!" She picked up the bottle of Chianti, turned it upside down to get the last slosh and the dregs. Wineglass in hand, she sat back in her chair and listened intently, her brow furrowed, as she strained to pick up the buzzing of the cicadas underneath the English and German voices.

"What would I do for a living?" Tim said as he polished off his *ragù di cinghiale*. His voice was deadpan, as it often was. Alison looked at him sharply to see if he was joking.

"We'd figure it out!" Her tone was imploring but also commanding. Tim settled the bill, and they headed out to the rental car. It was one of those marriages in which the wives always drive. Alison backed the car around in the narrow dirt parking lot, slamming on the brakes at the last minute to avoid an orange-and-white cat that darted out from the back door of the restaurant.

The question of educating their children abroad was not a new topic. It was a conversation Alison had had repeatedly with Tim about different countries, different languages. Sometimes it seemed as if anywhere would do, Copenhagen to Cartagena. Since their honeymoon a year ago, though, she'd been focused on Italy. That trip had been more peripatetic—they had been to Venice, to Florence, to Puglia. The point this time around was to really get to know a place.

The *agriturismo* was called Monteferallo. It was an eleventh-century castle southwest of Siena. When the paying guests drove out from the city after a day of tourist-ing, they would glimpse the crenellations on the rather short, squat tower from several kilometers away and, beyond them, the dark green forest of the Montagnola, and they would feel mollified, despite the fact that Luigi Ruggeri, the owner of Monteferallo, was slow to address plumbing issues and provide replacement light bulbs, that he hosted no welcome cocktail parties on change day the way other places were said to. There had been an issue with the booking agency when Alison informed them that they would be staying for ten nights only, arriving several nights into the first week. She had called, rather than e-mailing, in order to practice her Italian. "No, it is not possible," said the agent, who met Alison's quite passable Italian with halting, heavily accented English. Blushing and apologizing in her Tribeca kitchen, Alison hastened to explain that of course she would *pay* for the full two weeks, to which the woman had replied disgustedly, "Well, yes, signora. In this case, it is possible."

One didn't stay in the castle itself, of course. A long, low brick building housed three "touristic apartments," as the website called them. Three or four rooms apiece, they were furnished half with Ikea and half with Victorian-looking antiques made of dark wood. In a modern touch, on the back of the building, glass doors had been put in that opened onto little terraces. The terraces in turn looked out onto a large, square horse paddock. On the front-door side of the building, a gravel courtyard established a connection between the apartments and the castle itself. This close to the castle, one could not really take it in. One was aware only of a plain but forceful overshadowing high above the arched, centuries-old oak doors. Crunching barefoot over the gravel to the pool, Alison would stop and admire them—the heft of the weathered wood, the black, medieval-looking hinges. The pool was set in a sunken grass garden bounded by a row of cypress trees. Beyond the trees were a few hectares of vines; beyond the vines, a copse of olives that climbed a short, lumpy hill to a wood. Gunite did not seem to have come to Tuscany (the pool's siding was plastic), but no matter, Alison liked the 1970s feel of it—of the rubber-slatted chaise longues, the white plastic picnic table with the somewhat ratty umbrella that stuck when you tried to open it. "There's nothing I would change," she declared on a note of triumph to Tim as she toweled off after her first swim. And for at least a few hours, until she saw the horses up close, it was true.

Truth be told, Tim was a bit of a liability when it came to penetrating to the heart of the real Europe. He never tried to pass as anything but what he was: a bespectacled attorney who'd grown up in southern New Hampshire, the son of high-school math and music teachers. He would enter foreign shops, restaurants, museums—on their honeymoon, a Venetian newsagent where Alison had spent the better part of a week insinuating that she was, if not a local, then at least not an American—and say clearly, "Excuse me, do you have the international *New York Times*?" When they traveled, Alison often wished that she were alone and free to let people assume the wrong thing. Then, a couple of days after they arrived at Monteferallo, her wish was granted: Tim was called back to work over the weekend. Startled, Alison listened to him arranging to fly Monday morning from Florence to London, where the firm had an office. His flight left at the crack of dawn, so he got car service from

Monteferallo to the airport, but Alison promised to pick him up at Amerigo Vespucci upon his return Thursday night.

She had planned a spate of outings for the two of them. She'd read up for the trip, as she always did. Her Blue Guide was stuck with Post-its, the passages underlined; she could tell you the difference between the Giotto and the Duccio Madonnas and the names of the two Piccolomini popes. But a heat wave that descended over the weekend radiated on into the week. On Monday, she barely managed to drag herself to Sant'Antimo and back. On Tuesday, she drove to Murlo, where she lasted forty-five minutes in the Etruscan Museum before begging a guard for a cup of water. In her datebook, Wednesday was marked *Long Day: Siena!!!,* she recalled unhappily, waking at dawn on top of the coverlet in the simply furnished room.

The heat seemed to cast a spell of idiocy over everything— or to potentiate the spell of idiocy Europe cast over you, Alison thought, spilling ground coffee all over the counter when she tried to extricate it from the soft packaging and pack it into the finicky little Moka. Infuriated, she put the thing on the stove, pulled a robe over her T-shirt and underwear, and went barefoot through the glass door out onto the little patio. The patio had a teak table and two matching chairs; a lemon tree in a terra-cotta-colored pot divided it from the next apartment's terrace. Wanting to block the sun the day before, Alison had wondered if she would be able to rotate the plant even a half-turn; she'd tried and, in her surprise, said aloud, "Oh my God, it's *plastic!*" She sat down to wait for the whistle of the coffee, feeling peevish and foolish. The old, stooped man who worked on the estate finished watering the huge potted lemons that lined the gravel driveway just inside the gate and was now walking in her direction, dragging the hose. He reached the paddock gate and stood, filling the trough that was affixed to the fence there. In the far corner of the enclosure, the two horses bestirred themselves and came slowly toward him, raising clouds of red dust. With her ears laid back and her teeth bared, the bay mare herded the brown gelding. Their manes were long and scraggly, and the gelding's ribs showed in a way that suggested persistent underfeeding. The mare was old and swaybacked and walked on her heels, as if she had foundered. It was their feet Alison had noticed up close. They were grotesquely long and starting to curve, the walls of the hooves split by dramatic cracks.

Alison had a habit, when protesting an injustice, of ostensibly speaking to herself but raising her voice so that someone— in this case, the old man who'd been out raking; the German family who was occupying another one of the apartments— might hear. It was the same tone in which she said, of a favorite store, "How can it be closed? It was never closed on Sundays before!" and "You're *welcome!*" if someone for whom she held a door walked through without thanking her. "Criminal!" she had declared of the horses on her first day at Monteferallo. "Criminal to treat animals like that!"

The old man disappeared, dragging the hose. He returned a few minutes later driving the three-wheeled Ape with a bale of hay in the back, which he proceeded to fork over the fence. He watched the horses eat, and when the mare raised her head, moving her jaw in a circular fashion as she labored to chew the hay, the old man reached over the fence and rubbed her forehead with his outstretched fingers. His hand continued to make the caressing motion for a moment, even after the mare withdrew her head and went back to the pile of hay. From several days' observation, Alison knew that the horses came this way only to eat and drink. The rest of the time they stood in the corner farthest from the tourist apartments, where shade might have been had there been a single tree in the paddock. They stood nose to rump in the unforgiving sun all afternoon as flies congregated around their eyes. They switched their tails but in a desultory manner, as if they had given up trying to be comfortable and were only enduring—the flies, the heat, the dust.

"Why doesn't he build a barn for them?" Alison had said plaintively to Tim the day they arrived. She was referring to Luigi Ruggeri, the severe, aristocratic-looking owner of Monteferallo who had come out to greet them with diffident courtesy when they'd pulled in and had not been seen again. Edgy from all the coffee she had drunk to combat the jet lag, she refused to be placated by the gift basket of wine, olive oil, jarred tomatoes, and bread Tim discovered in the kitchen. "Something simple! A three-sided structure, just for them to get out of the sun!"

"Hmm."

"Or at least buy some fly spray, for God's sake! It's cruel!"

Tim had been sitting on one of the kitchen chairs, lacing up his running shoes. He listened and then pushed his glasses higher up his nose, took his cell phone, and went for his run. He had mapped out a three-mile circuit: over the bridge by Il Girasole, down the road, veering left up the hill—away from the ruined church there, which was said to be the best local example of the Romanesque—around to and through the little village that overlooked Monteferallo, then back down to join up with the long cypress alley home. "There was a farmer on a tractor plowing, and he stopped the tractor and watched me go by," he reported when he got back, panting as he caught his breath and chuckling. "Just sat there and watched." And the next day: "A car slowed down and some kids laughed and waved at me, and a dog from the village followed me the whole way home. I couldn't get it to turn back!"

Later they saw the dog, a fawn and white setter type, wagging its tail outside Monteferallo's massive wrought-iron gate. And later still they saw the old man coaxing it into the Ape, apparently to drive it home, while the Ruggeris' hunting dogs and the Doberman who guarded the place at night went crazy barking in some internal courtyard Alison and Tim couldn't see. "He's got the run of the town," Tim said approvingly.

Saturday was change day for the apartments. The quiet, self-sufficient Germans departed, and two new families arrived, one English, the other English-Australian. As long as Tim was there, Alison hardly noticed the other guests. But the moment he left, they permeated her thoughts. Here they all were in Tuscany, surrounded by what one of the guidebooks called the "unparalleled treasure of a millennium" as well as the most beautiful countryside on earth. Yet they seemed to feel no embarrassment about sitting around the pool all day. The two women had made friends—Edwina Charles, the Australian with the hard-dyed platinum hair who favored colorful caftans, and Katie Sobel, the trim, practical-looking Englishwoman with the brown, schoolgirlish braid. By eleven in the morning, they would be out there with the white wine going, passing it back and forth between the chaise longues, surrounded by a litter of magazines and fat paperback novels—that was Edwina; Katie did some sort of needlework, a crocheted bag always beside her on the chair. Their children, five in all, got up to games in the pool—Marco Polo and diving contests. Alison was jarred when they corrected her assumption that they were friends from home. "Oh, no—we just met by the pool!" Edwina said, sitting forward to spray sunscreen on her arms. "The children, you know," Katie added apologetically as the littlest one, a girl of four or five, came running up to her in tears.

Sometimes the husbands joined the women—garrulous, potbellied Mark, and Dom, who had a shaved head and was apparently in the army. Other times they stayed inside sleeping off hangovers. Lying in bed at night under the slowly rotating ceiling fan, Alison would hear the group of them laughing and drinking late into the evening, though courteously they congregated in the apartment that was farther away from hers. At midday, all four adults would pile into one rental car and drive somewhere for an alcoholic lunch. On Monday, Alison had returned from her tour of the abbey at Sant'Antimo to overhear them making plans in the courtyard. She went directly to her apartment and stayed there. She was afraid they would ask her to mind their children—they seemed like the kind of people who would make such a request as if it were no big deal. She hid inside her apartment until she heard them getting into their car. Then she came out and headed purposefully for the pool. She needn't have worried. They'd secured the Albanian woman to babysit—Vico, who cleaned the castle and the apartments. Alison's one direct interaction with the woman had made her recall an online review she'd read of Monteferallo: *Warning: These people speak NO English!*

Nor did Vico seem to speak Italian. She moved quietly about

the property, pausing in her work to observe the tourists with a sardonic smirk. When Alison tried to ask her how to use the oven, Vico had looked at her for a long moment, pointed at Alison's engagement ring, patted her own chest in an insinuating way, cackled, and said something indecipherable.

"If she takes them up to the tower and starts pushing them out, let us know, right?" joked the heavyset one—Mark—waving from the car.

Alison's face remained grave a moment too long. Then she said, "Right! Right! I'll do that! Ha-ha."

To Alison's surprise, Wednesday morning the Charleses and Sobels went off sightseeing, taking both cars, before she had finished her coffee. Through the front window of her apartment, she watched them leaving, Katie Sobel dashing back at the last minute and returning on the run clutching a stuffed rabbit, then running in a second time, her lips pressed into a line, and returning with a bottle of something that she shook—suntan lotion or bug spray.

Left to herself, Alison put off Siena. She sat beside the pool for hours, sheepishly at first, then vacantly, her eyes closed, the Blue Guide overturned in her lap. At noon, she was awakened by Vico, who informed her she was there for babysitting duty, as if she couldn't distinguish Alison from the other two women. When Alison explained that she wasn't needed—*"I bambini, non ci sono! Sono andati via!"*—the housekeeper looked suspiciously at her, as if unconvinced. Then she stood waving and calling loudly in Albanian to the two men working in the vineyard. The father and the son toiled there daily, moving slowly down the rows as they pruned the vines. "Agron! Agron! Agron!"

shouted Vico. After ten minutes of this, Alison stood up and said, "Well, seeing as it's no longer peaceful here, I guess I'll go to town after all! I guess I will go to Siena today, despite the fact that it's a hundred degrees in the shade!"

"Luigi! Luigi! Over here! Luigi Ruggeri!"

When Luigi spied the woman sitting alone at the bar, his mask of irritation softened to a more conflicted expression.

He had just come from lunch at his aunt's; she owned the building on the Piazza del Campo whose ground floor the bar occupied. Now he wanted to go back to his office and sleep for an hour with his feet up on his desk. Being called to made him feel exposed, as if someone had uncovered his plan of idleness, which, by reputation, he eschewed. But here was this woman, drinking alone at the bar in the worst heat of the day. Perhaps she had had a fight with her husband. Was she even staying at Monteferallo? The paying guests all looked the same; to be honest, he had trouble differentiating them. They were blowsy women who liked to drink and joke and sit by the pool. They could have walked in the woods, found the ruined villa a kilometer past the olives or the old couple's cozy restaurant on top of the hill. Instead, they stayed by the pool and ate at the restaurant across the bridge, where they were ripped off by Communists who gave them frozen *ragù*.

He put up his hand noncommittally. The woman was wearing a big straw hat. She rose and waved, gesturing to an empty chair. He hesitated. They liked to flirt with him, the women. A word from him—an exchange or two at the beginning of the week—went a long way toward keeping them happy. The joking with the guests, the keeping it light, did not come naturally to

Luigi, but if he chatted with the women, they did not complain about the lizards in the bathrooms or the chalkiness of the water or the lack of screens on the windows or the occasional mouse that was a holdover from the stable he'd converted into the three tourist apartments. "'*Ow* can I recommend you a place when I do not know you?'" was the stock answer he gave when they asked for suggestions of where to go, where to dine, what to see; he delivered the line with a self-deprecating smile that allowed him to make a quick escape.

But this woman—American, he recalled—momentarily disarmed him. She reminded him of another period in his life. Surprising himself, he went over, and when she spoke and gestured broadly, like a southerner, to the chair again, he sat down gingerly at the café table. He didn't sit facing her but rather turned toward the square, the way one sits when forced to share a table with a stranger.

"*Ti piace . . . ?*"

He raised an index finger and shook it. "No—no." He would have nothing to drink. It was far too hot to sit outside, besides which it was two thirty in the afternoon—no time for a drink. The tourists drank at odd hours—at any hour. Then, when it was finally dusk and time for an *aperitivo,* they would be getting the waiters to set up high chairs so they could feed their children.

"I was going to climb the tower," the woman said apologetically, indicating it across the square, "or at least tour the Duomo. But it's just so hot . . ."

At the bottom of the piazza, two mutts with bandannas around their necks were lying panting in front of the Palazzo Pubblico. A cluster of filthy tourists sat beside them right on the pavement, leaning against overstuffed backpacks, taking handfuls of food from plastic bags they passed around. "I guess they'll have to get out of the way for the Palio, won't they?" the American woman observed with a giggle. She began to talk about the horse race, engaging him flirtatiously.

A decade ago, when he was just out of his forties, Luigi had married an American woman like this woman—he had married one of the paying guests. Not one of the poolside drinkers, but the other type—they were not, after all, *all* the same. There was another, less common type, the serious women who came to Monteferallo not by chance, because La Bellina was booked, but on purpose, in order to see the church up the road, which they had studied beforehand. These were the ones who tried to read Dante in the original. Elaine, he recalled, had wanted him to settle an argument she was having with the friend she was traveling with about the Guelphs and Ghibellines. "Sarah thinks...but *I* think..."

How should he know?

Nel mezzo del cammin di nostra vita / mi ritrovai per una selva oscura...

He didn't admit it to Elaine, who seemed to assume he was some kind of authority by virtue of his birthplace, but that was all of Dante that remained to him. That and the three beasts—the lynx, the lion, and the wolf; he had liked that part in school...

It was Elaine who had initiated the custom of giving the guests a basket with a bottle each of the estate-produced wine and oil. It had not lasted—neither the marriage nor, at first, the tradition of the baskets on change day. After eighteen months, Elaine had screamed a litany of complaints at him—

she'd told him, "I'm losing my mind!"—packed up, and gone home to Connecticut, a state that he had been at pains to learn to pronounce. When she left, Luigi had immediately put a stop to the baskets, but the repeat guests complained and would go in search of him, thinking he had forgotten. Then the booking agent threatened to stop representing his property unless he made certain upgrades to the apartments.

With a discreet shift of position, Luigi observed the woman more closely. He took in her full breasts, deemphasized under a button-down shirt. He wondered if she was related to Elaine. He knew that it was unlikely and yet…just like this woman, Elaine had covered her face in sun cream and worn a large hat and sunglasses when she went to town. Just like this woman, Elaine had had points to make—many points. He sighed nostalgically, remembering Elaine's embrace that, in the impression it gave—of virginal innocence and deep cynicism combined—had been unique to him. He tried to picture the husband this woman had come with and failed.

"I just think the Palio is cruel!" she was saying, shaking the ice in her glass. "Not to mention dangerous. Running them around on the pavement. All those horses who fall…and the jockeys beating them and beating one another! Isn't it true, Luigi, that horses die in the race? Didn't I read that some-where? In my guidebook, maybe." She tried to catch his eye. "You probably think I'm ridiculous!"

"I?" Luigi smiled carefully. "No, no."

"About the Palio, I mean. A bleeding heart, right? Typical American." She smiled mischievously at him. "I know you're a big hunter…aren't you? Hunting! Shooting animals!" She mimed pointing a gun into the square. "I just hate all of it. Tim wanted to try and get tickets but I just said I have no interest in it—in seeing the Palio. None at all. I've seen the video—that was enough!"

"*Sì, sì,*" said Luigi, affecting a considerate tone.

It wasn't that he missed Elaine. He had gone back to his girlfriend Michela three weeks after she left. But he remained astonished that there had existed some other Luigi Ruggeri who embarked on that quixotic experiment. When he thought of that man, tears came to his eyes. So he sat for a few minutes with Alison Spalding, whose name he didn't know, and he indulged her questions about the Palio. He told her she must root for Torre and never—"not ez long ez you live"—for Oca (the Goose).

"Not as long as I live? Wow. All right, Luigi—that is certainly clear. That's very clear, Luigi Ruggeri. I'll remember that. Tower, yes; Goose, no."

Alison finished her Campari and soda in one gulp. "Now, Luigi, since we're talking about horses—while we're talking about the horse *race*, I mean—" She shook her glass, fished an ice cube out of the bottom, and popped it into her mouth, sucking on it as her eyes scanned the square and she searched for the right words. In her moment of hesitation, Luigi took his leave. He slipped away into the crowd. Flirting with an attractive guest was perfectly entertaining. But the plumber to whom he owed money had appeared in the square. He was gone before Alison could say, *Aspetta, aspetta!*

Then it was Thursday and Tim was due back. In the afternoon, when she returned from town, where she'd at last done the Duomo tour, Mark Charles hailed her as she crossed the courtyard. "Where you off to lickety-split? Come and have a drink!" He was in swim trunks and flip-flops, carrying glasses and a sweaty bottle of wine wrapped in a dish towel. The women, she could hear, were already poolside. "Stop! *Stop!*" one of them cried, not speaking to her children but reacting to something outrageous the other had said.

"I wish I could! I've got to go get Tim at the airport." Alison frowned at the affable man as if she expected him to contradict this, let her off the hook. "Well, maybe just one."

"Yeah, have one," said Mark, flip-flopping companionably across the gravel. "Hell, I need one for those roads!"

The two women, Katie and Edwina, had deserted their pool chairs and were sitting under the umbrella of the plastic picnic table. The German family who had preceded the Charleses and Sobels had eaten lunch there every day and lived on in Alison's mind. The two adults and their three children—a teenage boy and girl and a younger girl—would appear midday carrying out linens from their apartment, pitchers, cutlery, wine, platters of meat and cheese, salads, condiments, a loaf of bread. Passing them to go for a swim the day she arrived, having lunched on three cappuccinos and a gas-station chocolate bar on the way from the airport, Alison observed the older boy and girl straightening a tablecloth from opposite ends while the mother instructed the younger girl in slicing a tart. Since then, the table had stood empty except in the afternoons when Mark Charles had a solitary cigarette and drank a bottle of beer there, turning over the pages of a tabloid newspaper.

"Alison!" Edwina stood and waved. "Come sit with us! Come sit in the shade."

"There we go!" said Katie, picking up her chair and moving it to the side so Alison could squeeze in.

"Someone take these so I don't finish them," Edwina said, holding out a bag of chips as she resumed her seat. She was wearing her usual bright caftan and had slides on her feet. "Alison, please, finish them!"

Mark pulled a polo shirt over his paunch, but Dominic remained bare-chested as he uncorked the wine and poured out glasses at the other end of the table, his expression inscrutable behind reflective sunglasses.

"Cheers, m'dears!" said Mark.

"To Tuscany!" Alison added impulsively.

"To Monteferallo!" said Edwina.

"Heaven on fucking earth!" That was Mark again. "We went round all the vineyards yesterday," he said to Alison from the head of the table. "Bought a bunch of cases to take back."

"Yeah," said Edwina, "which I'm sure we'll find they sell at Tesco."

On the grassy stretch at the end of the pool, the Charles and Sobel children were darting and dashing around the yew tree. It was some game that looked like a combination of freeze tag and capture the flag but involved screaming *Buona notte!* when you caught someone.

"Bone-uh no-tay, you!" Katie included Alison in her put-upon glance. "Little monsters, aren't they? Hope they're not ruining your holiday."

"Oh, no! Not at all!" Robotically, Alison accepted another handful of potato chips from Edwina. "Though I guess I have been a bit stressed this week!" She had spoken unintentionally loudly; she gulped some wine. "You think Europe's going to be so relaxing, but when you actually get here, there are stressful elements. I ran into Luigi Ruggeri on the Piazza del Campo yesterday, and I was all set to ask him about the horses. I mean, I started the whole conversation in *order* to steer it around to the condition of the horses—"

Behind her, Mark put chummy hands on her shoulders. "It's your vacation, darling. You've got to relax."

"He's right, Alison!" Edwina said. "Mark's right. This is your time! You've got to enjoy it!"

"It's hard when you're on your own," Katie said sympathetically. "Dom's away for months at a time with the army."

There was a slow, rhythmic crunching on the gravel. They all peered back at the castle. The old man was out, doing his evening watering. He stopped and yanked a kink out of the hose, dragged it toward the paddock.

Now, keep quiet, Alison told herself, but a moment later, she blurted out, "I just wish those horses had a way to get out of the sun! It seems cruel!"

To her surprise, Edwina took up the remark. "Isn't it just awful? We were talking about it the other day!"

"Were you?"

"Poor things."

"I just don't understand why he doesn't build a barn for them! How much trouble would that be? I was thinking we could all—"

"It's a shame," agreed Katie.

"We could all—"

"Well, now." Mark gestured toward the paddock with his glass. "Not the easiest thing to get a building permit round

73

here. You would have had to apply in the early Renaissance. You can't go throwing up structures."

"Oh, Mark—typical man! She means the principle of the thing. It's not nice!" said Edwina. "It's—"

"Let me tell you what really gets me," Alison interrupted. "I think this might be the worst thing of all—"

"Have some more vernaccia, Alison," said Mark, topping up her glass, "and let your troubles cease," just as Dom cleared his throat theatrically, jerking his head toward the castle.

Luigi Ruggeri had emerged and was striding toward the gate, trailed by the two black-speckled pointers. He walked with the authoritative bearing of a cavalry officer. Despite the heat, he wore a loden jacket and tall boots and was carrying a rifle.

"Can't you just die?" Edwina murmured, and she and Katie went into paroxysms of giggles.

"Dom!" said Katie, a hand to her mouth to stop laughing. "Go and ask him to have a drink with us!" She made a shooing motion. "Go on, now!"

"That man is criminally handsome," murmured Edwina.

"What do you think he's going off to shoot?" Alison had meant to make a joke, but the question came out stiffly.

"Tourists who misbehave," said Mark.

"Mark!" Edwina crumpled up the potato chip bag and threw it at him.

"Actually, on second thought, I'd rather not know," Alison said.

"I know what you mean," concurred Katie.

"I just hate hunting. Hate all kinds of it. Even the deer

culling, though they say it's necessary. I just wish there were some other way…"

"And that, my dear, is your prerogative," said Mark judiciously.

"Hiya, Luigi!" called Katie, waving.

"Do come have a drink with us, Luigi!" Edwina raised her glass as Katie snorted.

Urged on by the others, Dom picked up the bottle and a glass and trotted over the gravel barefoot, waving the wine. He slipped and nearly went down but managed not to, using the bottle as ballast. The others cheered. When the dogs merely looked interested and took a step in Dom's direction, Luigi spoke to them harshly. Alison flinched, turning her head to look at the children, who seemed to have exhausted the game and were now sitting in a circle in the grass.

Luigi declined the wine but, in his guarded manner, came over to say hello. Katie got up to greet the dogs, asking, "May I?" before she knelt down to stroke them. "What beauties! What absolute beauties you are!"

In respectful tones, the men asked Luigi about the hunting and shooting he did. "Do you get any deer this time of year or is it mostly small things—hare and such?" said Mark. Dom questioned him about the rifle, which was an old one.

"Now, Luigi," Alison broke in awkwardly. "You need to buy some fly spray for those horses! They have that in Italy, don't they? Fly spray? They're *miserable* out there!" She was met with a sea of bemused, though not unfriendly, faces and Dom's inscrutable reflective blankness. No one made a reply. "It's cruel, Luigi! It's animal cruelty!"

"Eh. Well, I—" began Luigi in his halting English as a phone alarm sounded.

"Sorry!" said Dom, jabbing his finger to turn it off. "Time to get the fire going. Still okay if we use the outdoor fireplace tonight, Luigi?"

"Oh my God!" Alison stared dumbstruck at her watch. She was aware, all at once, of the sun sinking over the cypress trees, the dwindling light around the pool. "I'm late! I'm late to pick up Tim! Oh my God, I totally screwed it up! Jesus!" She knocked over her chair getting up. For a moment she was paralyzed, staring blankly at the yew tree as she tried to understand how she'd miscalculated the timing.

"You want Dom to keep you company?" Katie offered. "He's amazing on these crazy roads. Lots of time in a tank in Iraq to practice, you know."

"No, no, that's okay, I—"

"*Tutte le direzioni!*" said Dom. "*Tutte le direzioni!*" They all laughed—even, after a moment, Luigi Ruggeri.

Alison gunned the rental car and cursed herself all the way to the bridge. She had only the little things left to prove anything to Tim…showing up on time. Trying not to cause scenes. A car coming toward her blasted its horn angrily. She had forgotten to turn her lights on—they weren't automatic in the rental car like they were in the station wagon at home. "It's not even dark out!" she hollered, eyes smarting. "So you can shut the fuck up!" The bridge was before her, then she was over it and whizzing by the restaurant, its terrace packed with diners.

At the end of the straightaway, the road forked, the narrower branch going up toward the village—Tim's jogging route—

and the main branch jackknifing down around the ruined church and on toward the Raccordo. As she slowed to make the switchback of a turn, she allowed herself to admire, just for a second, the rounded Romanesque apse, what was left of the campanile rising above it, illuminated against the darkening sky. *Unbelievable!* was her first thought as a pair of lights appeared in her lane—in her face! Although…why was she having to swerve so severely back to her own side? And now—now there was something before her. Was it a log she saw too late? "Aaaaagh!" It was as if someone was screaming. As she jammed her foot to the floor, she seemed to hear the sound of her own voice from far away. The right front of the car bumped over something with a quick up-down. For a minute she thought she had hit a child. "What the *fuck?*" The car came to a whiplash of a stop—she had forgotten to put the clutch in. Her hands were gripping the wheel. A few seconds ticked by. She was trembling, moving her mouth. She felt clearly that this, whatever it was, could not actually be happening—could not have happened. A toddler—a toddler would not be out on its own in the near darkness. Would it? She swallowed carefully, turned her head, and looked behind her. The car she had swerved to avoid had not stopped. It was away down the straightaway. In the dim red glow of her own taillights, a shadow moved low to the ground. It slunk away with an uneven, hopping motion—upppp-and-down, upppp-and-down.

Do you get any deer or is it mostly small things—hare and such?

She snapped her head forward. She removed her hands from the wheel, rested them in her lap. A moment passed. She looked around again—all around herself, squinting up at the jagged outline of the campanile; craning her neck to see the lights of the village above and behind her; staring, finally, past the church at the blackness where the woods filled in.

Upppp-and-down...uppppp-and-down.

She seized the wheel and closed her eyes. She put her forehead down, rested it for just a second. She desperately wanted to go to sleep. The wine had made her so tired. Slowly, blearily, she raised her head...she couldn't just drive away!

But when another pair of lights appeared, coming over the hill from the Raccordo, then briefly dipping into the black, she turned on the car, threw it into first, and did just that. She drove away as fast as she could, racing through the gears to make up time.

There was nothing she could do. Nothing she could do. She lay rigid beside Tim—incensed when she heard him start to snore. What on God's earth was she supposed to do? This wasn't her country! She was only passing through! After a moment, she rose and felt around for her robe.

Standing at the top of an exterior set of stone stairs, she banged on the door. This was the side of Monteferallo where the tourists never went. She could hear the Doberman going crazy barking somewhere inside. "Luigi? Luigi! *C'è?*" For the longest time, she pounded on the door, and no one came. Then at last, there were footsteps and the door opened. It was the old man—the worker on the estate. She explained in Italian that she had to see Luigi Ruggeri. *"Muy importante!"* she repeated several times before realizing she was speaking Spanish. After a few minutes, though, Luigi Ruggeri appeared. He looked severe, but in truth he had been fighting on the telephone with Michela and relished the interruption. "You wake my father?"

"Your—father?" She faltered.

"My father! 'E come and get me! What do you want?"

"Oh, your *father? Tuo padre?* I didn't realize that was your *father.*"

"Why you—"

She made a gesture to silence him. "I hit something! A hare or a boar! About this high? It limped away." On the landing at the top of the stairs, she imitated the halting, uneven stride. She didn't care how stupid she looked or that, behind his serious demeanor, he might have been laughing at her. "We stopped on the way home, but we couldn't see a thing. Not a fucking thing! It's a blind corner, you know—with the church—and the cars coming around...I even got out and looked, I swear to God! But the woods—we don't know our way around..."

"You kill him?"

"No, no!" Her voice grew shrill. "That's the whole point! I *didn't* kill it." She was crying—crying and overenunciating to make him understand. "It's *out* there, limping *around* somewhere! Bleeding to death. Do you understand? *Il sangue*...bleeding...I feel so bad! I thought you could go kill it! Can you please just kill it?" she begged. "Put it out of its misery, you know?" She mimed shooting herself, gun to her head.

"*Va bene, va bene*—okay!" Luigi permitted himself a small smile as he summoned the English word that he could use only ironically.

"You mean you'll do it?" Alison raised her teary face. "Oh, thank God. Thank God!" She clasped Luigi's forearm in her hands. "Thank *you,* I mean. Forget God!" She giggled.

"*Grazie! Grazie mille,* Luigi. I'm really sorry what I said yesterday about hunting—it's stupid, I know. It's asinine! I should just go become a vegan and shut up about it. That's what Tim thinks. You should talk to Tim! He finds me incredibly exasperating too!"

"I will get my gun."

"That's great, Luigi." She felt giddy now, as anyone who's been given a reprieve does. "That's really great of you. Thank you so much. Idiot tourists—I'm sure you're sick of us. But hang on a second—" she said as he began to close the door. "I should tell you exactly where I was. I had just gotten around the turn. It was heading toward the woods, I'm pretty sure—"

"*Ho capito,*" Luigi interrupted, waving her away. "I will go there."

In the morning Luigi planned to avoid her, but Vico kept him outside in the courtyard, pointing out a wasps' nest in the eaves of the tourists' roof she wanted him to get rid of. The American woman caught him there, as well she might; they were standing right outside her door. He kept the interaction short. "I got him," he said briefly. "Yeah? You did? But—what was it? You never told me what it was!" she cried as he strode away, pretending not to hear.

In fact, Luigi had gone nowhere near the church. He knew the woods there and he suspected that she had hit a badger anyway, not a *cinghiale*—or a porcupine or even a stray cat. He would take the dogs up later today or tomorrow if he felt like it. But the beauty of it was that he'd told Michela he could not come into town to see her after all. He had gone out—he stayed out the whole night stalking a *cinghiale* in the

Montagnola. He had been leaving corn under the rocks every night for the past few weeks, and the boar was now in the habit of coming around to rout at night. He didn't get him, but he would the next time, and indeed he did—he killed him a couple of nights later and made his father drive out with him in the Ape to haul him home, before the *carabinieri* could get him for illegally killing a boar.

It was a minor satisfaction in a week that had piled on hassles. Michela had accused him of canceling on her the one night in order to pursue an affair with one of the paying guests. It wouldn't be the first time! she said, over and over—*Non sarebbe la prima volta!*—until he wondered, aloud, what the point of life was with a woman like her. That same day, the day after the American had come to him with her incoherent request, the farmer from across the way paid him an unexpected visit. Brogi looked aggrieved and said he was looking for his wife's dog—the setter hadn't come home the night before. After a hesitation of no more than a moment, Luigi cut Brogi off and began to chastise the farmer. He told him he had to keep Enzo in the house at night, not let him go ranging around. The neighborhood was changing! There were people who would steal a dog like that; Brogi ought to know better. You couldn't trust anyone. He yelled at him and badgered him, calling him an idiot and a baby, until the old man left, throwing up his hands and shaking his head, half in tears.

Then Luigi went and got his gun.

He pulled smoothly into the clearing south of the church, the side with the scaffolding, where a mini-excavator stood, abandoned these last few weeks, who could say why. Luigi had no eyes for the faltering restoration, as his was not the only car parked at the church. For a moment he sat in his Fiat, staring straight ahead. Once in a while, a paying guest would ask for his money back. The reasons were usually obscure. A man from California claimed the pool was dirty. A Canadian couple complained of "tractor noise." Having composed himself, Luigi got out and closed the door. He cast his eyes up at the campanile, nearly white against the blue sky. The air was perfectly still. Then a sound asserted itself in the stillness, a slow *chink…chink*, like a stake being driven into the ground. When he listened, the noise stopped. Then it started up again. Now he could hear a voice—a muffled little scream—in time with the metal on rock, or earth. He walked quietly around the end of the church, pausing every couple of steps to listen.

In the shady corner formed where the nave met the base of the tower, a harried, red-faced figure raised the butt of a shovel over her head and slammed it down. Each time she struck the ground, a cry escaped her mouth. Luigi went cold. This was like nothing he had ever seen. Instinct told him to keep silent—to sneak back to the car. He began to edge away, but she snapped her head dumbly in his direction, like an animal caught in a sudden light. Her mouth opened, and her face contorted into a look of such venom that Luigi thought of his gun, lying useless on the back seat of the car.

"You!" she shouted. She threw the shovel down. She advanced toward him, wiping her hands on her thighs. She was pointing—pointing right at him, stabbing the air with her forefinger. "You lied to me!"

"Madam, I do not think so," began Luigi, but an appalling wave of fear and shame made it impossible to go on.

"You said you would kill him, and you never did!"

Was that all? He wanted to laugh with relief, but, just as so often in his dreams when he was summoned for punishment, he could not speak a word in his own defense or move a muscle to run away! She came right up to him—exceedingly close! There was a black smudge on one of her cheeks, and her hair stuck out around her face. She was so close he had to force himself not to tilt his head away from her.

"*I* had to do it!" she shouted. He felt her spit on his face! "Do you hear me?"

"I—"

"*I* had to put it out of its fucking misery!" She jerked a thumb behind her. "I had to bang its head in with a fucking shovel!" Involuntarily, Luigi's eyes strayed to the dark corner. "All you had to do was fucking come and shoot it, and you couldn't even do that! What kind of a... what kind of a person—"

The American woman's voice broke. Her shoulders slumped. She turned away from him, a hand to her forehead. She began to cry, heaving for breath. "The poor little thing! Poor little dog."

Luigi pursed his lips. This he had seen, many times. These people—they had their own problems, and Monteferallo wasn't what they expected...Without thinking, he reached out his hand. He patted her shoulder gently, and she made a slight turn toward him—seemed to accept his comfort, to be glad of it. But when he took a step closer to gather her in his arms, she spun away as if he had struck her. "Oh my God! Oh my God! You have got to be kidding me!" She strode toward the cars. Now she stopped and turned—she gesticulated wildly at him. Her face went red as a tomato. She was shouting and shouting—

throwing her hands up in the air. Something about Italy. He kept his eyes on her face and tried to look concerned.

"You've ruined this country for me, Luigi! Do you hear me? *Ruined* it! Italy could have been my favorite place on earth. But thanks to you, I'll never, ever come back here! Do you hear me? Not as long as I live!"

As she reached her car, she burst into tears. Fumbling for the handle, she got in and slammed the door. He followed at what he hoped was a respectful distance. She turned the car on, but when she went to back it out, it stalled. She got it going and reversed, but when she shifted to go forward, it stalled again. He eyed her through the windshield. Now she merely looked miserable and defeated. As she drove away, he averted his eyes. He pretended to be studying the campanile.

Around the back of the church, Enzo lay in the shady corner where he had dragged himself. Luigi surveyed the body of the dog. His hind end was completely torn away, the two legs not distinguishable one from the other but a filthy, bloodied mess that the maggots had gotten to. Foam still leaked out of his mouth, but Enzo was dead, having had his skull bashed in. That reminded Luigi of something—he glanced around and retrieved the shovel. It was heavy, a good tool. He was surprised that no one had stolen it from the worksite before now. Then he recognized it—it was his. That she had come prepared to do the job made him stop where he was to get his bearings. It was like when he went up to their bedroom after Elaine left him—driving off after a fight they got into over Easter lunch— and found the wardrobe empty of all her clothes.

*   *   *

Luigi went home and got his father, and the two men drove out in the Ape with a tarp and gloves and loaded the corpse into the back. Vico's husband and son, out spraying the grapes, spotted them coming back, driving up the hill beyond the vineyard. They came along for the fun of it. They were all in a good mood, enjoying a bit of action. Agron, the son, was fighting fit—he dug the grave with his shirt off and at the end, showing off, pried out a boulder and dropped it on the spot.

Feeling conciliatory, Luigi drove to town that night and took Michela to the *contrada.* Over dinner, he worried aloud that the Albanians would tell Brogi; the family moonlighted for the farmer from time to time, doing seasonal work. Michela assured him they would not—Agron and the father didn't have papers, she reminded him, only Vico did. They would never tell. *"Allora,"* Luigi said, taking a small sip of red wine and permitting himself a smile at the comical English word: "We are 'okay'!"

The Taker

A few weeks before my wedding, one of my friends told me, in the presence of my future husband: "I had a dream that you dumped Doug, and he was hitchhiking on the side of the road, all sad and lonely, with his thumb out, and you drove by in a fancy car and didn't stop to pick him up, and he was crying and running after you down the road, for miles and miles and miles, begging you to stop the car and take him in, but you just kept driving." She paused there. "In fact, you accelerated."

This was years before the term *microaggression* was coined, but later on, when it became popular, and "Conversational Don'ts" started to come across my social media feed, such as "Telling a person you are surprised to see them in such-and-such a setting," I would always mentally add, *Relating a possibly fake dream to a person in which the person figures unflatteringly.*

Before I met Doug, I had composed a list of requirements in a spouse. It wasn't a mental list—I had jotted it down on a

Post-it that I came across periodically, marking, e.g., a passage in *The Seven Habits of Highly Successful People* or clinging to an interior zip pocket of a faux-leopard clutch (I am not sure the fashion writers can justifiably claim that animal prints are ever "back," given that they never truly seem to go away). *Nice manners* was the sine qua non my eyes alit on most frequently because it was near the top of the Post-it—second only to *job*. By *job*, I meant something you put on a suit for—it was the '90s, and I wasn't having any of this tech-world no-tie nonsense.

In my early twenties, I had a fling with a guy who was getting an MFA in film studies and wanted me to shop with him for mock-turtleneck sweaters. "Shop with you?" I remember I asked him after a long pregnant pause. The subject of mock-necks swiftly died.

Going Dutch? No.

Sharing breakthroughs you'd had with your shrink? Goodness, no.

My nickname in college was "Picky," and in the group house I lived in, my then boyfriend used to have to come over when it was my night to cook. His specialties were fettuccine Alfredo and a beef and broccoli stir-fry. I toyed with dumping him senior spring, but I needed access to a car.

Cut to a year into my marriage.

Doug is gone at the finance job eighty hours a week. Jobless myself, I wanted at least to pick up his shirts for him, but whenever I went into the dry cleaner's, ticket in hand, and announced, "I believe you have some shirts for me!" the proprietor would remind me testily that they offered free delivery. From the man's passive-aggressive insistence on this point, I gathered that performing this service gratis truly mattered to him, so in the end I let it go. (Not to let him seize the upper hand entirely, I insisted on *light* starch and eschewed plastic and hangers in favor of the boxed option for shirts, despite the impression I had that the latter was not a true option but was there only to pad out the price list, as BOXED OR HUNG!—yes, there was an exclamation point on the sign—sounded so much more exciting in a choose-your-own-adventure sort of way than simply SHIRTS: LAUNDERED.)

I am talking about the time before Marcus came, of course. After Marcus, everything changed.

Before my friend Gillian sent Marcus to stay with us, I spent my time googling rescue dogs and obsessing over having bought the wrong couch. You think of blue as the most basic of colors, but it turns out to be tricky—it turns out to be cold. I also made a point of reorganizing the apartment a good deal in order to attain maximum efficiency in Doug's and my homelife: our closet; the spice cabinet; the books, though never by color—that, to me, is misguided. Sitting in the nail salon one afternoon—I stuck to a regimen of regular manicures and pedicures even if there were other things I felt like doing on manicure day—I read an article that said that busy couples should schedule sex, and while I could not claim to be busy in any broad sense of the word, an eighty-hour-a-week job in a Midtown investment firm certainly qualified Doug. I let him know that Fridays and Tuesdays would be our nights, with a free option for Saturday afternoon. Occasionally, when I reminded him about the Schedule, say, or noted that the spices were now alphabetized, with the exception of the star anise, which was too large to fit in its rightful place, between sage and tarragon, I caught Doug looking at me sideways, a bit like you look at someone who is making a scene in a waiting room, someone whom you might actually sympathize with if you were alone but vis-à-vis whom, since people are watching, you need to draw a line. Also, if I went out and left him alone in the apartment—a rare occasion, given how much he worked—when I returned, I would often find him playing such popular heavy-metal bands as Metallica, Black Sabbath, and Iron Maiden while slamming a fist into a long round pillow known as a yoga "bolster."

I have often asked myself in retrospect why I felt compelled to accept Marcus DiDomenico as a houseguest. On the isle of Manhattan, as everyone knows, it is an effort to let someone spend a single night in one's apartment, let alone an astonishing, unprecedented string of *eleven*. Doug and I were, as I said, newly married. We were living in a one-bedroom-plus-alcove that our broker had assured us could work as a nursery just as soon as we felt "the urge to expand," which, I took it, did not refer to the weight gain we newlyweds were likely facing as we started down the path toward middle age. In these intimate quarters, I didn't have room for anything but a close friend— Gillian herself, say, not her ex-boyfriend, this Marcus fellow whom I had never met. Which was not to say that he wouldn't be perfectly pleasant. But more to the point, I didn't have the *psychological* bandwidth to share my physical space. Everyone who had ever known me knew this and kept their distance. In college, I lived in a single. Afterward, I was never asked for a room or a bed. I was never asked for much of anything, though I spent long hours in our new apartment considering how I would make hypothetical guests comfortable and had already worked out exactly the traffic pattern that would be most commodious for everyone: I would shower at night; Doug would shower early; the guest would have coffee in his or her robe and then shower.

It must have come down to flattery.

Among my friends from college and from the early years in New York, there were those who had a nonstop stream of houseguests. I would ask them what they were doing of a weekend (just casually making conversation) and be told that Ronnie or John or Kimba Lee Downing or Beth G. or the Hanlons, after they spent a night in a Boulder, Colorado, jail, or Greta Weicker's sister, who was auditioning for the touring company of *Rent*—someone—was always in town, crashing for a few days. These friends were not better off than I, with more to offer in the way of accommodations. It was I, in fact, who had escaped the dreary, almost incapacitating penury of our twenties by marrying Doug. These friends lumped it with their guests—sharing bathrooms, of course, and beds, leaving keys with supers, making the guests take care of their rescue cats, car-walk their cars, even come down on weekends from "up-state" or "Mass." or "Syracuse" expressly to help them move apartments. We all moved constantly in those years, and two things these "friends" of mine always had besides houseguests (I am never sure with this particular group of peers whether to put that word in quotations or not) were rescue cats and people to help them move. No one had ever showed up to help me move. I had ridden in the cabs of trucks with crews of Israelis I'd hired on glib recommendations; in my more budget-oriented moments, I'd ripped tabs off Man-with-a-Van signs on telephone poles and, once, a Woman-with-a-Van sign; that mover turned out to be somewhat of a liability as she couldn't lift my flea-market urn turned planter, and I had to call in reinforcements, namely, a Man-with-a-Van. I'd been alone—metaphorically speaking—when the brassieres I stuffed into the box of cutlery because they were air-drying when the movers arrived fell out on the street and into the gutter. Still, I had a history with these friends, and I kept up with them in my fashion. I had invited them to my wedding, for instance. Doug and I got married young—the cutoff IMO was thirty—with bridesmaids and *engraved* invitations, not embossed, and I remembered eternally and with perfect clarity who came but never sent a present. Of course it was this very same group of friends with the rescue cats who couldn't be bothered to ask where Doug and I were registered, who found the idea of registering comical, found weddings comical, found the words *bride, groom, mother of the bride, canapés,* and *receiving line* all comical. When some of these friends eventually did marry, at the tail end of their thirties, the ceremony was in a field somewhere, and despite our twenty-year history, I was never invited.

Gillian Dunn was outside of this circle of mostly college friends and acquaintances. She and I had met at a party on the Lower East Side and hit it off. I'll just admit up front that it was our fault Pataki got elected. We were drinking in a room with the TV on when the election results came in, blaming "low voter turnout" for Mario Cuomo's loss. We looked at each other, cleared our throats, and moved away from the television into another room. Later—unrelated to the New York governor's race—Gillian moved to Paris. A few months after that, she e-mailed me with the name of an old boyfriend—American, she hastened to clarify, in case I thought I'd have to entertain *un gentilhomme français*—who was moving back and needed a place to crash for a few days. *Of course!!* I wrote back, after waiting half an hour to give the impression I was thinking it over, though in fact I had already rushed ahead to ordering sheets from the Company Store for the foldout love seat—overnighting them in case the friend's dates changed.

I wrote, *Of course!!* and added breezily, *Let me know when he's showing up!* and then, *No, it's totally fine with Doug! He won't care at all!*

In fact, I wondered briefly if my husband would care—if indeed he would be put out by having a guest in the one-bedroom-plus-alcove when he returned from his exhausting, exacting job and by having a stranger walking through our marital sanctum/bedroom to get to the foldout in said alcove. My response to these doubts was to delay telling him until two nights before and then spring it on him as a *fait accompli.*

And so, a few weeks later, on a gray and drizzling early-spring afternoon, I was buzzing up the first nonfamily houseguest of my married life.

In a stroke of bad luck, it was the cleaning woman's week off, so I had done a surface cleaning of the entire apartment. I'd also laid in a supply of groceries—coffee, fruit, individual yogurts, and things I am told people like, such as prepared salsa and the ubiquitous hummus and "guac." The night before, now that Doug knew about our guest, he had obligingly hung up eight pictures under my direction. They had been sitting on the floor, leaning against our bedroom wall since we moved in. Eager to help, I threw myself into the task, letting Doug know when a print was not straight despite what he thought, saying, "Don't you want to use a level? I'm sure it would be better!," having him raise them one inch, lower them two, align them with the molding of the doorway, then align them purposely *not* with the molding of the doorway as I tried to recall whether there was a rule about this. I mused aloud, but only briefly, about whether prints were even really what we ought to hang on our walls at all. At some point I heard Doug saying under his breath that he had to go to bed or he wouldn't be able to work in the morning at the job that paid for our lives, and I said, a little tearily, "O*kay*—jeez! I'm just trying to make the apartment look nice for our guest!"

Other than the decorative question of prints, only one thing frightened me in the minutes before I opened the door to Marcus—it had been worrying me all week. In the few months that Gillian had been living in Paris, she had gone completely French. That was one of the reasons she felt so confident moving over there—she knew she had it in her to go French and she had done it, seamlessly, from what I could tell. The language, yes, but also the driving, the parking, the fashion, and the cooking were immaterial to her. She learned all of the idioms as if she'd spent her whole life, instead of about a month and a half, stuffing trash into tiny cans and eating with her fork turned down. Guessing at the life Marcus had led with Gillian, at what my future guest was accustomed to, instead of suggesting that Marcus and I order a pizza (Doug was working late, as usual), I had run out as in the old, single days and done the equivalent of buying a fluted tart pan and four new spices. (I still owned the actual fluted tart pan from years—and many, though exceedingly intermittent, tarts—ago.) Finding it difficult to focus on, I rarely cooked for the two of us. I had spent either a week or three and a half hours—depending on whether you count time spent in big-picture contemplation or time crunching actual recipes—deciding what to cook for this, our inaugural guest-dinner. I had rejected fish as too tricky and pasta as a cop-out, meat as too stagy and sycophantic, and vegetarian as too Moosewood/rescue-cat. For a long while, I stared at the suggestion for "An Academy Award Buffet" in the *Silver Palate Cookbook*. But in the end, I was left with chicken. Surprisingly, I had always been able to make a decent roast chicken; my college boyfriend showed me how when my housemates did a faux Thanksgiving our senior year. I copied Dean's instructions exactly, down to the type of pan he made it in, a glass Pyrex baker; I would not have known what to do with a ceramic or metal one. I made it with lemon and tarragon on a bed of onions and celery, and I cooked it on high heat till it was past done. I had the very index card I'd written the recipe down on in college and I always read and repeated Dean's ingenious insight as I cooked it: "People like overcooked fowl"; it was a kind of calming mantra. This was the only dish you could say was part of my repertoire—let's face it, it *was* my repertoire. So, after much, in retrospect needless, contemplation, I decided to make the chicken for Marcus DiDomenico. I had to go to three stores to find tarragon, as if there'd suddenly been a run on it. I did the chicken and rice and a green salad with toasted walnuts. I was all a-dither and to calm myself down, I blasted whatever was on the stereo, which turned out to be a disc from Doug's twelve-CD compilation *Led Zeppelin: The Definitive Collection*. I ran around shout-singing the various songs, and as I was belting "Many times I lied," I burned the walnuts and had to throw them out, and the kitchen smelled of burned nuts when I opened the door even though I'd been darting back and forth alternately opening the windows to get the smell out and closing them because it was so cold inside my teeth were chattering. I had not finished the vinaigrette when Marcus arrived, but I tried not to become mentally paralyzed by this fact. I tried to look on it with equanimity.

No doubt, I thought hopefully, *he will want to wash up.*

"I was going to get flowers, but I had too much stuff!" Marcus pronounced when I opened the door on him and his three enormous suitcases. Marcus DiDomenico was tall—six two or six three—and good-looking, by which I mean *good-looking;* you could have set him up on a blind date and told the other party that he was "good-looking," and you would not have been lying or even exaggerating.

"Let me help you with those!" I said for some reason, and proceeded to drag the large roller bag inside and then go back for the others as Marcus glanced around the apartment with a bemused expression and then went over to the pair of windows opposite the door. "Back view," he said with a wince when he lifted the shade and peered under it. "Too bad. But still—" He gave me a commiserating smile as I muscled and kicked and humped the last suitcase—an oversize duffel bag—over the threshold. "It's great to be back in New York."

I made some appropriate introductory remarks and showed him the alcove where he would be staying. "Make yourself at home!" I said and continued on in that widely recognized "hosting" vein. "I got out that luggage rack for you...the window sticks, but if you give it a good push, it'll open right up!"

As I gave my welcoming spiel, Marcus, who had sat down on the alcove love seat that would fold out later into a bed, closed his eyes. He inhaled long and deep through his nose, as if he were starting to meditate. Ujjayi breathing it is called.

"Yeah, so we'll all be sharing a bathroom," I said faux apologetically to Marcus. "But Doug leaves pretty early, so it should be okay." When I mentioned Gillian ("Wow, I miss her since she left. She and I—"), my houseguest took another long breath in through his nose, opened his eyes, and fixed me with the same look a young man had given me who dumped me in a diner just before his pancakes and eggs came. He even said more or less what the dumper had said: "I can't deal with this right now."

I had my line all ready. "Welp, I'll leave you to it!" I said snappily, and I called back over my shoulder, "Dinner'll be just a minute!"

It was clear I was going to excel in this hosting role. It was simply that I'd never been given a chance! After Marcus, I'd probably have a long string of guests—people would call me, impromptu, from Penn Station: *Hey, I know this is last-minute, but any chance I can crash?* Then people would probably start to refer houseguests to me of two or even three degrees of separation: *I know you don't know Veronica well, but her brother's ex-girlfriend and I . . .*

I hustled around in our little kitchen, my heart beating erratically, making the salad dressing. I was so nervous my hand shook when I stirred the mustard into the olive oil and vinegar. When I checked the chicken, I saw to my dismay that it was browning far too fast. Just my luck! I ripped off a piece of tinfoil and covered it, patting it down around the sides of the Pyrex. Still, Marcus did not appear. I had put the cutlery, flatware, plates, and glasses on the folded-down Duncan Phyfe table we kept pushed up against the south, windowless wall of the combo living/dining room. This was so that when Marcus asked what he could do, there would be a nice, contained task for him of setting the table. But Marcus DiDomenico, I realized when I finally walked back through our bedroom to the alcove to check, had fallen asleep.

He slept and slept the way you can only sleep when you're indulging the jet lag instead of fighting it. This is a strategy I do not recommend. In fact, it is one of my core principles to never give in to jet lag, but clearly Marcus and I did not share that value. I turned the oven off. I killed an hour, during which time I walked back to the alcove twice more and listened to his snoring from outside the door, clearing my throat loudly the first time, the second time pretending to trip and calling out "Oops!" and "Damn it!" I turned the stereo on at full volume "by accident." "Whoopsie-daisy! Sorry about that!" I shouted. Eventually I carved the chicken, mistakenly hacking away at a thigh bone till I found the cartilage. When at last, around nine thirty that night, I heard Marcus moving around in the alcove, I jumped up and reheated everything, ferrying dishes back and forth from the counter to the microwave. Marcus emerged in cutoff sweatpants and a Hüsker Dü T-shirt with a royal case of bed head. I blushed, waiting for him to offer to help—listening for my cue to set him at ease, to say dismissively, "Don't worry about it! Just relax!" Instead, he went and examined our bookshelves. He frowned as if something there unsettled him. "Can I borrow this?" he said, taking down my high-school copy of *The Great Gatsby.*

"Of course!" When he didn't thank me—or respond at all—I cried, "I've read it! Keep it as long as you want!"

We sat down to dinner. "Will you do the honors?" I said, handing Marcus the bottle of red and then, with a flourish, the corkscrew.

He put the bottle in his crotch and tugged, then stood up and yanked. Half the cork came out; the other half had broken off and disintegrated into the wine. He splashed the wine into the two glasses I'd put out, filling them up to the tippy-top.

"That's plenty!" I cried. "Jesus."

"Why? Is there something wrong with this?" he said, taking a sip just as I was setting him at ease by saying, "Don't worry about the cork—it'll be fine!"

Staring blankly past me, Marcus shoveled food into his mouth for several minutes while I chattered away, filling the silence. First I told an anecdote about me and Gillian back in the "old" days. But I didn't want to be rude and keep the conversation focused on me, so I said, "Gillian tells me you're here to interview for a job? What sort of work do you do?"

He dragged his eyes away from the wall, chewing. "Me?"

I nodded, smiling warmly. "Yes! You. I mean—you! What do you, ah, do?"

"For a living?"

"Yup! Yes."

"I'm a management consultant."

"Ah, o*kay!*"

"Yeah, I've got this interview tomorrow…" He frowned. "Ugh! I'm so sick of it!" he spit out suddenly.

"You're—"

"I'm sick of all the fucking bullshit!"

"Ah, the bullshit! I see, I see…well, I certainly hear that. From what I understand—"

"Do you have shoe polish in the house?"

Keys in the door jangled at this point, and Doug came in. "What's that smell?" he called from our tiny foyer as he hung up his coat on the Ikea coat tree that he had assembled two nights ago after we retrieved the flat pack from the closet where it had lain for months. He came into the living/dining room, stopped, and did a double take. "Whoa—you cooked? No *way!*"

"It's just chicken," I said evenly.

"Sweet! I didn't know you were gonna *cook!*" Doug turned to our guest. "Hey…Marcus, right? I'm Doug!" They shook hands, and I felt a little flutter of pride in my husband. I would have to strive to make sure Marcus did not feel left out, did not feel himself to be a third wheel in our happy-young-marrieds' nest while he was alone and jobless—for the moment, anyway.

"Hiya, Doug! I heard about you! How's it going, man?"

"You want a beer?" Doug asked Marcus as he went to the fridge.

"Um, actually, there's red open," I said.

Marcus stopped his glass halfway to his mouth and placed it to the side of his plate. "Yeah, a beer'd be better," he said, and a look of misgiving crossed his face. Doug handed him an IPA. "Thanks, Doug! I appreciate it, man. Really glad you showed up, Douggie boy." He pointed at the glass of wine and looked at me. "You want the rest of this?" It was the first time I noticed that he didn't use my name.

"That's okay," I said primly. "I'm fine."

*   *   *

Historically speaking, Doug likes no one. He is quick to smile and quick to laugh, but his easygoing demeanor masks a dismissiveness the likes of which I have never encountered in another person. So when he came to bed at midnight after talking and laughing with Marcus for more than an hour—while I lay awake, hearing just enough of every conversation to want to dispute its premise—I said, "Wait a minute. So you *like* him?" Marcus had not come into the alcove yet but I had made up the sofa bed for him so he wouldn't have to stumble around in the dark.

"Oh God, no," Doug said, but he chuckled to himself as he unbuttoned his shirt and placed it directly into the dry-cleaning bag—a house rule established by me a few months previous—and when I asked what was so funny, he said, "Sorry. Sorry! Just this thing we were—never mind."

In the morning, Doug left early as he always does and I made coffee. Then, odd as it was, there was nothing for me to do but wait for Marcus to wake up. I had no plans until beginner yoga at eleven—I had been attending the beginner class for three years but still held out hope I would master the chaturanga and one day advance to "Open" level. I sipped my coffee and read the paper and did the crossword, and as I was looking up from writing *rube* in 19-across, I heard something move in the combination living/dining room and I screamed.

"Whoa there, Nellie!" said Marcus, who had evidently been sitting there the whole time. When I could breathe again and could assess the situation, I understood that he had slept on the living-room sofa, resting his head on the decorative pillows and using the decorative-accent-color (raspberry) pashmina throw as a blanket, which he now had wrapped around his naked shoulders and chest.

"Little too early in the morning to get excited!" he said. "The morning sets the tone for the whole day."

"So, you…you slept out here?" I had jumped to my feet when he startled me and remained standing.

Marcus dog-eared the page of the book he was reading and tossed it aside. I saw that it was my high-school copy of *Gatsby*. He stretched, lazily scratched his stomach, and hooked the raspberry pashmina under his armpits. "Yeah. The other room was kinda bumming me out, so I came out here. This couch is rock-hard, though—yikes! You might want to have it restuffed."

"I love this couch!" I said hotly. "Although," I admitted, "I should never have bought it in blue."

"Blue's tough," Marcus agreed. "I have this friend. Kelsey, see? And she's awesome at decorating and colors and everything, so wherever I live, I just have her come over and tell me what to buy and where to put it, and my apartments always look awesome."

"This is in Paris?" I said.

He gave me a look. "Naw. Just forget it."

The pashmina still around his shoulders, he padded over, barefoot, in his boxers to the coffeemaker on the kitchen counter. I didn't want to stare at his naked torso so I glanced at his legs. He had long, bandy surfer legs covered in golden hair, and surfer feet—long and curved—and he walked with that surfer walk, as if everything underfoot was ouchy hot sand. At any moment, I was sure, he would absently, conceitedly, touch his stomach and use a word like *gnarly* or perhaps *nasty*.

"Oh—I can get that," I said as I quickly and bodily blocked his access to the mugs. "Here you go!" I plucked one from a row of them hanging on little hooks underneath the kitchen cupboard and handed it to him. "Do you take milk or sugar? Or we may have some cream in the fridge. I'm not sure. Doug likes half-and-half but he gets his coffee at work, so..."

He shook his head balefully. "Oh no, you don't. No fucking way."

"Okay, well, for breakfast, there's yogurt, or I can make toast—"

"The dairy industry is up to some *nasty shit*. I gave that crap up years ago. You kidding? I don't go near that lactose crap." He overfilled the mug, and the coffee splashed out onto the counter. He leaned the pashmina into the spill and wiped with it using his elbow. Then he turned, bent over the coffee, and sipped off the top, no hands.

I cleared my throat and said tightly, "Okay, well, anyway, for food we've got—"

"Hey!" He straightened up and the pashmina slipped off and puddled on the floor, leaving him naked except for his boxers. "Can I use your phone?"

"Of course!" I said between gritted teeth as I snatched up the throw from the floor. "There's one in the alcove. I mean, if that's *okay*," I added sarcastically, recalling his dislike for the alcove.

He looked surprised but then the surprise melted into a different expression—an expression of commiseration. He grasped my shoulder. "It's o...*kay*. It's okay. It's gonna be all right, okay?" He put the coffee down on the counter and stepped behind me and began to knead my shoulders and the base of my neck. "Man, you're so fuckin' *tense*. You gotta relax! Life's too short!"

He took his coffee mug down the hall, spilling all the way, and after a couple of minutes, I heard him shouting and laughing. "But that's in*sane!*" Later, as I made my bed, I heard "Fucking kid. Ding. Me!" And when I stood outside the alcove one last time, he was saying, "Uh-huh, yup, okay, got it," in the tone of someone who is jotting down instructions. I poured myself another cup of coffee and drained it, tidied up the living-room sofa, tried to sponge the coffee off the pashmina, and plumped the decorative pillows back into place. After forty-five minutes my houseguest was still on the phone. After an hour, I picked up the receiver in the kitchen and said, "Wait—what? Marcus? You're still on? Sorry! I hadn't realized that. I can make my call later."

"Oh," he said coldly. "Okay."

I went to beginner yoga to give him time to get out of the apartment, and in class I stood in the back. It wasn't the usual teacher but some overly ambitious young woman who heckled us through thirty or forty sun salutations. By about minute twenty, I started saying audibly, "What's she trying to do, kill us?" and "As far as I know, the Ramamani didn't believe in *torture!*"

Fearing over-caffeination, I lingered at the studio, nursed a lemon verbena in an off-brand coffee shop, and ran a couple of errands. At this point, I figured, there could be no doubt that Marcus would have left the apartment. He had mentioned a job interview. It was after noon now. Job interviews struck me as morning kinds of appointments generally speaking. It seemed safe to return. If he was still there...well, tough luck. It was my apartment. I wasn't going to be guested out of it.

When I stepped into the apartment, I tripped over something and fell to the floor with my shopping bags. It was Marcus's huge roller suitcase, now, inexplicably, back in the living room, and not only back but open on the floor and spewing clothes and shoes. Before I could get off the floor, Marcus appeared, still naked but for his boxers—a new pair, I noticed, with a panting-beagle motif. He winced as if he were embarrassed to say what he was about to say: "Um...I never did get that shoe polish."

"I asked Doug!" I said, getting to my knees. "We don't have any here. He's been getting his done at work." I hesitated. "But you know what? I'll run out and buy some. It'd be good for us to have some around. What color do you need? Black? Brown?" I asked. "Cordovan?" I added for some shoeshine humor, which I don't think he picked up on.

He didn't answer this. "What size does Doug wear?" he asked.

"Eleven? No—eleven and a half." I got laboriously to my feet using the bags as ballast, then had to get back down on my hands and knees and finally lie down flat to retrieve an orange that had spilled out of one of the bags.

He addressed me as I was lying on the floor reaching under a chair for the orange. "Yeah? Those might actually fit."

"So, you need to borrow some shoes?" I said pedantically as I got to my feet.

"Only if you can find them in a hurry. Kinda...chop-chop situation, you know?"

I found it highly amusing that he didn't think I was up to

this hosting gauntlet he had thrown down. I left the groceries on the counter and, still in my coat, went to our bedroom closet and immediately laid my hands on Doug's backup pair of dress shoes.

"Voilà!" I said triumphantly, handing them to Marcus, who disappeared into the alcove. I unpacked the groceries, leaving him alone to get ready, but when he didn't emerge after a few minutes, I walked back to the bedroom and called, "So what time is your interview?" Nothing like a little passive-aggression to get people to do your bidding, I figured, taking a page from my dry cleaner.

He opened the door, dressed in a rumpled suit with no tie as of yet. Just as I was making the mental leap of conceiving of management consulting as a more casual industry than I had envisioned, Marcus replied, "One p.m."

"One?" I was aghast. "But it's a quarter of! One?" I repeated. "Is it close? Are you kidding me? How far do you have to go?"

He closed his eyes and did the long, slow nose inhalation again.

"You're gonna be *late!*" I said remorselessly. There was no use sugarcoating it. Despite my limited success in the workplace (sex on the copy machine: xeroxed cheeks), I had gathered that corporate entities cared about things like punctuality. "You at least can't be *late!* Jesus Christ!"

Marcus put his hands over his ears. He sat down on the previously scorned love seat and began to sing, "'Happy birthday to you! Happy birthday'—" I gripped one of his hands and pried it away from his ear.

"You are going to miss the fucking interview!"

"'Happy *birth*day, dear'..." He stopped and pressed his fists to his eyes. "My suit!" came a muffled cry. "It's fucking wrinkled!"

"Oh my *God!*" I got the address out of him—it was somewhere near Columbus Circle.

Of *course* I told him it was far too late to think about ironing. Of *course* I explained that it was better to be fifteen minutes late in a rumpled suit than half an hour late in a pressed one, but in the meantime the argument itself was wasting precious time. He stripped down to his shirt and boxers and I flew off with the jacket and pants. The ironing board was jammed into our one storage closet—though less jammed since we'd relieved it of the flat-pack Ikea coat tree—and when I yanked it out, a dozen things fell to the floor: an abandoned needlepoint project of a spouting whale; *The South Beach Diet: Supercharged;* a number of translucent plastic shoe-organizing drawers, currently empty, so not organizing anything, contributing, in fact, to the disorganization. The irony of this did not escape me, but I had time only for ironing just then, and not for its literary word-cousin. I set up the board in the hall outside the alcove and barked out instructions as I ironed: "Get your tie on and comb your hair!" When I checked the bottom of the iron to make sure it wasn't too hot, I burned my fingers. I started on the pants, going, "Ow! Fuck! Ow! Fuck!"

Thank God I am a wonderful ironer. I can do pleats and Peter Pan collars and ruching like nobody's business. The rescue-cat crowd, needless to say, lacks this skill entirely—a fact that brought a condescending smile to my lips when I recalled it. They have no use for an iron and ironing board; indeed, many of them do not own either, as I discovered when I wanted to quick-press a pocket flap on a cotton blazer I had worn to a garden party in deep Brooklyn without realizing the pocket had dried folded.

By 12:57, Marcus was dressed. He had neglected to tie his tie and I had to do it for him. Perhaps he thought he would charm the interviewer with a rumpled louche appearance, but I felt this strategy was a risky one. I'm not sure what he had done in the several minutes in which I ironed the suit, to be honest. As I was reaching up and standing on my tiptoes to push the knot into place, I felt his lips on my hair; however, I ignored this because I had noticed that it was the same tie as one of Doug's. I addressed him frankly. "Are you a graduate of Davenport College at Yale University?"

"No," Marcus said.

"I see."

"Shit! Shit! Shit! Shit!" he exclaimed, feeling in his pockets. "I don't have any cash for the cab!"

You will have gathered that this was before New York taxis took credit cards or used phone apps or allowed any form of payment other than cash. I had previously been caught out myself in a similar fashion so I called reassuringly—I was already halfway to the kitchen—"It's okay! I keep a stash of cash handy for just this reason!" I pressed a second twenty-dollar bill on him after the first, just in case he got into traffic or got lost. He could thank me and repay me later even if—as I feared—he did not get the job.

He rushed out the door and I flopped down onto the sofa as if I would never rise again, but just as I was lying back, putting my feet up on the coffee table, and reaching for *Gatsby* so I could smooth out the dog ears—not to worry, I planned to put a pencil in the book to mark his place—there was a peremptory knocking on the door.

I let out a scream of agitation as I rose from the sofa. When I opened the door, he didn't look me in the eye but only stood there mumbling to himself, "I can't do this. I cannot do this! I haven't interviewed in years. Years! Do you hear me?" This last question was directed to himself, and I wondered passingly whether he suffered from what used to be known as multiple personality disorder. That would explain a lot, I thought. A hell of a lot. But I took hold of his shoulders and physically spun him around and pushed him down the hall.

I trailed him right to the elevator. I was about to go back but thought better of it and waited until the elevator arrived, my arms folded across my chest in a classic pose of defense while he quietly cursed himself: "You fucking idiot. You fucking, fucking, fucking idiot. You always *fucking* do this! Sometimes I really hate you!" The elevator came; he got in. And the doors closed on Marcus DiDomenico staring forward with a frightful intensity.

After organizing Marcus's suitcase sufficiently so I could close it and drag it back down to the alcove, I lay comatose on the couch. In point of fact I was waiting for the cable guy, who, two hours after the appointed window, still had not shown up. My houseguest, I understood now, was in a precarious mental state. Fragile to begin with, he was clearly losing his shit. I considered calling Gillian to discuss him, but I couldn't muster the energy and, truth be told, I shied away from talking about someone behind his back when he was still under my roof. I only had to get through another day or two—he was slated to leave on Tuesday or Wednesday, latest. As the day wore on, I considered the kind of pressure he was under and I steeled myself to listen supportively when he got back. As the day wore on, I worried he was lost. As the day wore on, I opened the door several times and listened, as if I would hear him lurking in the hallway or taking the back stairs up. I worried that he had been so agitated he had blown off the interview and was now too ashamed to admit it. I worried all kinds of things.

At five thirty, I called Doug. After some preliminary back-and-forth, I said casually, as if it were an afterthought, "It's a bit weird, but I haven't heard from Marcus all day." I explained how he'd gone off, late and worried, for the interview. "I guess I thought he'd either be home by now or else I'd hear from him. I'll have to figure out a way to leave keys because"—I sounded the kicker triumphantly—"I actually have plans tonight. I'm meeting Kelly for drinks." Kelly McMahon was a childhood friend of mine, briefly in New York for an accountants' conference. "It's been on the books for weeks."

"Oh!" said Doug. "Oh."

"What?"

"Well, it's just—*I've* heard from him. He and I—"

"You've heard from him?"

"Yeah!" said my husband. "He called me to see if I wanted to meet up for a drink."

"He did? You mean tonight?"

"Yeah—we're meeting in an hour."

"Oh. Okay. I see," I said. Then I added, "Great!"

"I figured you'd be glad if I got him out of the house for an hour."

"For sure. I mean—definitely. *Definitely.*"

"Cool. Apparently the interview went really well, by the way—they want him to come back for another round."

"Really?" This gave me pause. "I'm kind of surprised, to be honest, given how late he was," I said by way of explanation—not wanting to impugn Marcus's actual skills as a management consultant, of which I had no knowledge.

"Weird—he didn't mention that," Doug said. "Told me he cabbed over a couple hours early so he could walk around and check out Radio City."

I hesitated. "Well—have fun tonight!" I said.

"You too!" said Doug. "Tell Kelly I say hi!"

The truth was, despite having grown up on the same street in the same small town, Kelly and I didn't have all that much to say to each other. Before becoming a certified public accountant—a "CPA," as they call themselves—she had spent several years in a cult to which she had twice tried to recruit me. I could see a couple of benefits of being in a cult—any cult, let alone this particular cult, where the food, apparently, set the standard for farm-to-table—but as I said to her then, "I guess I prefer life on the outside." Since the year she was deprogrammed, I had felt it would be untoward to go there conversationally; at the same time, I didn't know much about accounting. My usual opener when we met for drinks was "So...how are things at the Big Five?" I could never remember which big firm she worked at but I wanted her to know that I knew she was not working at a small accounting firm that people had never heard of. She, meanwhile, with surprising tenacity, usually spent these *rendezvous* trying to elicit an explanation from me as to what I did all day. I sometimes felt she had been sent by our small hometown to extract information about me and bring it back. Tonight, feeling my time management was my own business, I kept ordering appetizers whenever she lobbed a direct question, and pretty soon we had eaten three sliders apiece, a basket of popcorn shrimp, and a mini–goat cheese soufflé and I felt I had to shut it down or be compelled to order the ubiquitous hummus or "guac," which I suspected would be of an inferior quality at the Irish pub where we had met.

As I came up the stairs to our floor, I could hear uproarious laughter coming from my apartment. My smile may have been a bit uncertain when I went in, given that I'd pictured awkward conversation over takeout while they watched the basketball game on network TV, the only channels we got at the moment while we awaited the arrival of the cable guy. But whatever confusion I had about what the two of them were finding so incapacitatingly funny was cleared up the minute I shut the door behind me and heard Doug saying, "So, Donnegan just says, 'Oops!'" I was tempted to turn around and go right back out, maybe kill an hour drinking alone at a dive bar—that's how much I didn't feel like hearing the Donnegan story.

I stepped into the room from the foyer. Marcus was lying facedown on the floor in his now extremely wrinkled suit pants and shirt, also now untucked and unbuttoned, laughing so hard his ribs were shaking. He was *pounding* the floor. "Oops!" Doug repeated. "So the guy just says, 'Oops!'" Doug made a visible attempt to control himself as I came in, but when he tried to say, "Hi, hon," he cracked up, took a sip of beer to stop himself, and proceeded to spew it all over the coffee table where my guest-friendly large-format photography books were stacked. Empty beer bottles were strewn across the coffee table and kitchen counter and there was a stack of pizza boxes on the floor by the couch.

"Looks like you guys are having fun!" I said, shooting dagger eyes at Doug. "I guess I'll just crash early."

"Sounds good, hon!" Seemingly chastened, Doug asked how my drinks with Kelly were.

"Well, you know Kelly. She—" I started, but I was cut off by Marcus erupting again into his guffaw.

Struggling to speak, he pushed himself to sit up. "So he just—he just—he just says, 'Oops!'"

I stood there waiting for him and Doug to stop laughing hysterically.

When I could get a word in, I said angelically to Marcus, "Hey, how'd the shoes work out, by the way?" I was so prepared to say *It's okay, really—don't worry about it* that when he opened his mouth to speak, these words were out of my mouth before I heard what he was actually saying, which was "To be honest, a little tight. Turns out I'm more of a twelve than an eleven and a half."

My response sat strangely in the air, especially given how solicitous of our guest I had been thus far. "Well, hon, it's not okay if he can't walk in them!" Doug said awkwardly.

I looked at him in silence. I headed for the hall, then paused. "The cable guy never showed." I added pleasantly, "I waited all day."

"He didn't? Damn it!"

"I guess I'll just have to wait tomorrow too."

"Sorry, hon," Doug said, looking glum.

"Oh, hang on a minute, Doug," Marcus piped up. "Did you say cable guy? As in Time Warner?"

Doug nodded. "Yeah, he was supposed to come and replace the router."

"Oh, I talked to them! A couple of times!"

"Oh, did you?"

Marcus laced his fingers together, turned his palms out, and stretched his arms up straight. "Yeah, it was some call-waiting bullshit and I was on to Brazil and I couldn't deal, so the third time, I just blew it off."

"Sure, sure," said Doug. He took a sip of his beer. "No big deal!"

"Ah-ha-ha-ha-ha-ha! He just says, 'Oops'? Ah-ha-ha-ha-ha-ha."

I retreated stonily to the bedroom, where I lay awake fuming. I hated the Donnegan story—hated it. It was an offensive story. But to be honest, that wasn't the reason I hated it.

Mike Donnegan was one of Doug's suite mates in college and one of the three guys he shared a low-rent apartment with in his two years in the city prior to business school. A pithy fellow by all accounts, Donnegan was known for many *bons mots*, including his oft-quoted TGIF variation: "I'm gonna rock out with my cock out." Donnegan had bedded so many women in his teens and twenties that "Wait, did you do Donnegan?" was an icebreaker that could be heard in the early '90s among women meeting one another at parties from SoHo to Doormandy. Donnegan was so promiscuous, there were even rescue-cat women who had slept with him despite the wide chasm between Donnegan's and their sensibilities. Indeed, the very best parties of my twenties were the ones that both Donnegan and the rescue-cat crowd attended. Suffice it to say simply that at these parties, the shit went down. But back to Donnegan. Donnegan had been at it so long he *couldn't remember* how or when he'd lost his virginity. He was like one of those kids who grow up on horse farms—there had never been a time when Donnegan couldn't ride. In college, Donnegan had famously gone from one woman's bed to another's in the same night *and then back again*. In his twenties, Donnegan had conducted an affair with a married B-list celebrity that made the *Post* and the *Daily News*. And so on. But to get to *the* story: In college, Donnegan liked to get young women to have anal sex with him—it was a known predilection he had, among many others. One young woman was, despite Donnegan's many charms, resistant to the idea. So Donnegan, coming home one night crowing—Donnegan always crowed, gleefully—shared a piece of advice with the guys: "Yeah, so you just pretend you wanna do it doggy-style, and then you go, 'Oops!'"

That was the story.

It was a stupid story. The very stupidest. The anatomical facts did not support it. But neither the rapey *dénouement* nor the suspension of disbelief the story required was the source of my irritation with the Donnegan story. The secret reason I loathed it was that my husband loved it. Indeed, Doug looked for any opportunity to recount it. Every retelling was nails on a marital chalkboard for me. I began to fantasize about ways to get him to stop telling it. For instance, I knew he would not have told it if *I* had slept with Donnegan. The story would, in that case, have been too close for comfort. But by the skin of my teeth, I had not slept with Donnegan. Indeed, the night I came closest to sleeping with Donnegan was the night I met Doug. So there was no way to keep Doug from telling it and telling it and telling it, to not hear the admiring chuckle that punctuated it, to not note the blissful, vicarious chortle of every married man from FiDi to Upper Fifth who lovingly repeated the Donnegan story.

A little while ago I came upon a list that I'd made—on a piece of paper; it was before anyone used a phone for that kind of thing—entitled "The Top Ten Transgressions of Marcus Di-Domenico." His failing to thank me for the use of my husband's shoes and for ironing his suit pre-interview, his blowing off our cable appointment, which took seven days to reschedule—none of those even made the list. The list, you see, was composed entirely of incidents from the *second half* of Marcus's stay, all of which vanquished the first-half offenses so thoroughly as to make them seem like sun salutations in beginner yoga. The second half of his stay officially started the Wednesday after he arrived. I cleared my throat as he was pouring his coffee and asked him what time he'd be heading out. "Oh, you mean to get some air?" No, I said, and reminded him that he was leaving later that day. "Ha! Right! What? How would that even work?" was all he said. "Doug and I have plans to go to Monster Trucks Friday night!"

In the second half of his stay, Marcus violated the guest/ host code in so many ways, it is hard to recall all of them. He took daily baths and failed to drain the water. He ran the dishwasher with dishwashing liquid in it. He exploded his takeout Chinese in the microwave and left it there. He opened the bottle of Romanée Conti we had put away for when our first child was born and used it to cook with but then fed the dinner he made to a homeless man who lived on our street. After he gave the man dinner, he brought Beppe up to our apartment to take a shower. "But..." I murmured. "I don't have any towels..."

"He can use my towels," Marcus said tartly. "You fucking liberals—you're all the same. You preach charity but then you don't want a guy like Beppe here to get your towels dirty!"

I did as I was told; I always did now. I had become, in the space of a week, like one of those mothers of four—chaos didn't faze me. I could get dinner on the table in half an hour. I no longer complained about the faults I found with my cleaning woman; Marcus didn't like faultfinding. "I say, just do it your fucking self and shut up about it!" But that wasn't all. Another day when Marcus came home—apparently from an interview, but I had given up trying to parse how he spent his days—he yelled from the alcove where he still stored some of his things even though he didn't sleep there that he needed me. "I'm cooking!" I called back. "I don't want to burn this!"

A few minutes later he appeared in the kitchen, naked but for a towel around his waist. "Look, I'm in pain here. I need you to rub this on my back and you're like, 'I'm cooking'? What the fuck?" Without another word, he handed me the bottle of Bengay.

"Where do you want it?"

"Lower back."

I started to rub it into his back.

"Lower...lower! Jesus—" He craned his neck around. "Are you hearing me?"

"I've reached your towel," I said stiffly.

"Oh my God! Are you one of these people who're so uncomfortable with the body, you can't cope with a flash of butt crack?" He whipped off his towel and I found myself massaging the Bengay into his butt cheeks. I tried to rub it in with a confident hand.

Wouldn't it be nice if Doug arrived home just now? I thought. Though in truth I wondered if it would have any effect on him—I wondered if he would even notice. For days now, I had seen my husband down a long narrow tunnel; I had no direct access to him at all, no line in, and the distance never shortened. He had started sleeping in the alcove so as not to awaken me when he came to bed at one or two a.m. In the mornings, I slept as if I were the one who was hungover—he would be gone before I could rouse myself. Needless to say, the Schedule had fallen completely by the wayside. When the cable guy finally did show up, I brought him a seltzer water, offered him bridge mix, and hung over him as he worked, but the moment he finished installing the new router, Marcus arrived home and engaged him in a conversation about upgrading our package to include HBO and Showtime. And by that point, I had to get dinner started.

I dreamed that I was in a desert being pursued by monsters, and Doug was so far ahead of me, he couldn't hear me screaming. When I awoke, I was silent-shouting his name. I had started to leave early for beginner yoga—to walk the streets for hours just to be out of the apartment. That morning I dressed in my athleisure outfit and made coffee, working as quickly and silently as possible, but I dropped a mug, and a minute later Marcus sat up on the sofa in the combination living/dining room. "Listen," he said. "It's kinda been a while for me ... and I was thinking maybe you could just, you know ..." He turned his palms over and gestured to his nether regions with both hands.

I said: "Are you asking me to perform fellatio on you, Marcus?"

"Fellatio!" he fairly screamed. "Who said anything about fellatio? Jesus! I was just thinking maybe a hand job!"

As he was saying the words *hand job,* the apartment door banged open, and Doug stood there framed in the doorway. "I forgot my keys," he said. He turned to Marcus, who suddenly looked rather sheepish. "You're going to have to leave, Marcus," said Doug.

"But she—"

"You've overstayed your welcome," my husband said distinctly. "And now it's time to go."

He waited while Marcus took a twenty-minute shower, singing the chorus of "Rhiannon" over and over, each time saying, in place of *heaven,* " 'Would you stay if she promised you *leather?* " We had a polite conversation, Doug and I, while we waited, about the many couplings and breakups Fleetwood Mac had experienced. We waited while Marcus tried on and rejected different outfits, then while he made calls and stubbed his toe on the alcove foldout. "Ow! Motherfucker!" we heard. "Time to throw this piece of shit *out!*" At last Marcus emerged, wearing his suit jacket over short running shorts and a T-shirt, grasping Doug's Yale tie in his fist. "Okay if I borrow this, Dooger?"

I was about to protest, but Doug put up his hand to stop me. "Sure, Marcus. Just take it."

He escorted Marcus down to the curb after heaving two of his three huge suitcases out to the elevator. I went back to the alcove and surveyed the room. He had left a wine bottle with a centimeter of wine remaining in it; *Gatsby* splayed open with, I saw, picking it up, half of the title page torn off (I later glimpsed it in the wastebasket—he had used it to throw out gum); and a piece of my monogrammed stationery on which he'd made a flowchart that mentioned *new york, tangiers,* and the words *distance to border* without capitalization or punctuation.

Doug didn't come back upstairs after seeing Marcus off. He went right to work, so I didn't see him till that night. I spent the day in one of those detached yet meditative states they're always talking about in yoga but that I'd never been able to come close to achieving. I didn't think of much at all. I tidied and cleaned and made a simple supper of sausages, lentils, and steamed broccoli. Doug came home, and we ate it in silence, alternately sipping from our wine and our water. About half-way through the meal, we both suddenly spoke at once.

"I really hope he didn't forget—"

"God, I wish I'd told him—"

That was sufficiently embarrassing that we both drained our wine in a hurry. And after another glass or two, I began to giggle for no particular reason and found I couldn't stop. Doug did a Marcus imitation that was so good, it was uncanny—he got the stretch and the walk and the stare. Like an old married couple, we didn't start making out till we got into bed. "Now, according to the Schedule, we're not actually, I mean *technically,* supposed to—" I couldn't stop myself from saying, but I found I was too distracted to finish the sentence. That's when I heard Doug say, "Oops!"

We Don't Believe in That Crap

In a previous life, long before he met their mother and they were born, the girls' father had been military—air force. Retired military had the right to shop at the army base one town over from Peckton. Everything was cheaper there than at the V and C, the grocery store in town. On Saturday mornings the girls went food-shopping at the commissary with their mother, and on the way home they stopped at the Moores' to give Ma her cigarettes and drop off the ironing.

Because he had started over, he was older than their friends' fathers—a new wife, a new state, a new career, them. He had drawn a line between the first and the second lives. He trained as a civil servant—hung up his uniform. The girls brought the blue dress hat to school for show-and-tell and the rolled-up citation for bravery that he had never framed. He did not speak to his three grown children from his first marriage—or, rather, they did not speak to him, blaming him, the girls gathered, for some obscure technicality, though he was quite obviously the most blameless person one could hope to meet. He did not tell stories about the old days except once in a while he would say mildly that in Okinawa after the war, you could golf all day for three dollars, and a beer was fifty cents. He no longer golfed. He no longer drank. A phrase the girls knew from a young age was *cold turkey*. Linda liked her wine, and they threw parties, but he never again touched the stuff except on Sundays at the altar rail. Even if you were an alcoholic, you were allowed to kneel down and take the Blood of Christ. "Your father's an Episcopalian," she would tell the girls. "I'm not much of anything—though I'm very spiritual—but it's important to your father." It didn't *seem* particularly important to their father, who never spoke of God and certainly never mentioned Jesus Christ; going to church was just something he did. Like shining his shoes, rising at five every day and cooking breakfast, making the queen-size bed with corners so tight, a staff sergeant (the idea was) could bounce a quarter off the top sheet. When friends came over, the girls would show off the perfect bed, but then Kristin Coon, a neighbor they didn't much like but wound up playing with, said disgustedly, "Your *dad* makes the bed?" After that, Natasha, who was dark-haired like their father, shut it down. She told Becky, who was two years younger and fair like Linda, "We're not going to show kids their room anymore." And when Becky forgot, she elbowed her and said meaningfully, "Remember."

The Buick had a sticker on it that showed you were allowed onto the army base. When they exited off the traffic circle and pulled up to the gate, a young soldier snapped to attention from the side of the little guardhouse. Today, as always, he not only lifted the bar and waved their car through but also saluted the three Bradford females. The girls' father had retired as a major, and the sticker was a certain color to indicate that he had been an officer. In the back seat, the girls had sat up and gone quiet, anticipating the salute. Natasha, who was eight, gave a small nod back. Linda smiled sadly, took her hand off the wheel, gave an embarrassed little wave, and said, "Poor kid, standing out there all day. Probably enlisted because there was nothing better to do."

They drove past rows of barracks and the strip mall that housed the PX, then pulled into the commissary and parked in front of the low ugly building. Inside the commissary was a different world. It teemed with people. Under the fluorescent lights, men, Black and white, shopped alone in army fatigues and tall, black lace-up boots. They carried their baskets soberly, picking up Styrofoam packages of meat and frowning at the labels. "We don't buy our meat here," Linda would often announce in a stage whisper. Natasha steeled herself for the comment, but today, mercifully, she didn't say it. They worked their way down the cereal aisle, Natasha pushing the cart, Becky finding the items on the shelves and tossing them in, lickety-split. Toward the end of the aisle, where the sale items were, a chunky baby was sitting in the front of a shopping cart in a diaper and T-shirt. It was kicking its bare chubby legs through the slots in the cart and laughing. A teary, snot-faced boy of about three was standing up in the cart itself. Natasha glanced at Linda, who looked stricken. "I would never let you stand up in a cart!" she hissed.

"Pop-Tarts, Pop-Tarts, Pop-Tarts!" the little boy was wailing to a woman in curlers and a shapeless housedress. "I want Pop-Tarts!"

"Pop-Tarts are *delicious*, aren't they?" Linda said to him. The mother in curlers looked up from examining the bashed-in boxes of sale cookies. An identical friendly wariness came over her and the little boy's face, as if they weren't sure what they were dealing with. "I just love Pop-Tarts!" Linda smiled her kindness-giving smile. This was a lie—Natasha averted her gaze from the falsehood. Linda had never bought Pop-Tarts in her life. She didn't know what they tasted like. The only reason Natasha knew what they tasted like was that Kristin Coon brought them on the school bus and would sometimes deign to give her a bite for nefarious trades, such as Natasha's letting her give her an Indian sunburn. Natasha never let Kristin make Becky do anything, though. Becky couldn't stand pain; it always surprised her. She hadn't come to the realization yet that it was part of the deal.

"Bye-bye!" Linda beamed at the boy. "I hope I'll see you here again!"

The boy nodded sheepishly as the Bradfords moved past him, Natasha maneuvering the cart. "Pop-Tarts!" he cried piteously. "I want Pop-Tarts!" The woman in curlers turned and swatted him so swiftly that none of them saw it coming. The little boy fell back into the cart, howling. "You're gonna shut up or you're gonna go home, d'ya hear me?" Walking quickly away, Linda blinked rapidly, pressing her lips together. "You're not gettin' no Pop-Tarts!"

Natasha wheeled the cart to the end of the aisle, where Linda batted the air with her hand, let out a long fluttery breath, and said, "I'm fine, girls. I'm going to be fine. Tashie? Are you okay? Becky?"

When they had gotten all of their groceries, including the carton of Carleton cigarettes for Ma, Natasha identified the shortest checkout aisle. Their mother greeted the young man who was standing at the end of the conveyor belt. The Commissary hired adults with Down Syndrome to do the bagging. "Hello, Timothy!" Linda said, beaming as she read the oversize plastic name tag. The checkout clerk, a thin, sallow-faced young woman with long, stringy hair, ignored them.

"Hello, missus," the young man said as he waited for the groceries to come down the conveyor belt. He wore a blue-and-white-striped cap like a railroad engineer's, and he touched it politely.

"Is that a trainman's cap?" Linda said.

"It's—it's an engineer hat."

"Oh, of course it is!" She slapped her forehead. "An *engineer* hat!"

"I have to bag the groceries," said the young man.

The last item the checkout girl rang up was the carton of cigarettes. "They're for my friend," Linda told her. "I hate supporting the habit, but I'm afraid smoking is my friend's only pleasure these days, and the cigarettes are cheaper here on the base, so I buy them for her. Is that hypocritical of me? I suppose that's very hypocritical of me. I'm supporting something I think is wrong."

The girl announced the total in a monotone.

Linda wrote a check, putting their father's military ID number on it. That was to show the check wouldn't bounce. Then she withdrew a five from her wallet and put it into the cigar box at the end of the belt next to where Timothy stood.

"Thank you, Timothy! Here is your tip!"

"Most people leave a dollar," said the young man, not looking at the bill.

"Well, I'm putting in *five* dollars! Do you know why? Because you did such a good job!"

"Most people leave a dollar."

"*Thank* you, Timothy! Thank you again! I'll see you next time!" She turned around to wave at him as Natasha pushed the cart toward the door. Natasha had already opened the bag of pretzel rods and fished out one for Becky and one for herself. They had one each now and they'd have one each in the car— that was all. After that, she wrapped up the bag tight-tight and stowed it down in one of the brown-paper grocery bags so it wouldn't open. Natasha hated things to go stale. At home she obsessively patrolled the kitchen for open boxes of Triscuits, ripped sleeves of Ritz and Saltines.

"Bye-bye!" Linda was still smiling and waving as they re-treated. The young man, intent on the next load of groceries coming down the conveyor belt, did not turn around. In the parking lot, as they unloaded the contents of the cart into the trunk, Linda put on her sunglasses because her eyes had filled with tears. "They can really have such productive lives," she said, her voice cracking a little.

The Moores lived in a cleared hollow that ran below Mashopee Road. Ma Moore had taken care of Natasha and Becky and a host of other Peckton children over the years. She still took in ironing but now Angie, one of her daughters-in-law, did most of it. There were two trailers in the hollow and three dilapidated houses, one with insulation instead of glass in the windows. They were occupied by various branches of the Moore family and their hangers-on. The kids from the hollow all got on the school bus at the same stop, on the corner of Mashopee and Hemlock—they climbed directly up the hill through the woods to get to it. They were often late; many mornings Natasha and Becky sat waiting in the school bus for one or another Moore-related kid to appear.

Linda took the dirt road off Hemlock. The pines yielded to raw dirt such as you'd see on a construction site. Ma's house was the first house you came to in the clearing, the two-story house. It had a downcast aspect, as if it were sinking into the ground, even though Clinton, one of Ma Moore's former foster boys, had redone the front porch for her last summer. Off to the side of the house was a three-sided barn whose roof was caving in. Clinton had turned it into a garage. Its projects spilled out into the driveway and yard—tires; sawhorses; tarps held down by rocks that seemed to be covering more piles of tires; a Cadillac sedan, rusting, up on concrete blocks, with its hood open. Ma had four children of her own and she took in fosters and runaways, so there were always teenagers hanging around, shouting as they screeched off in cars. Clinton himself was grown—he had quit high school; he no longer appeared on the bus. But such was his devotion to Ma that he had stuck around. He was out in the driveway today working on a motorcycle, his shirt off. He was leaning over the bike and didn't look up when they drove in, but inside the house a racket of barking started. A teenage girl they had never seen before was standing beside him, hanging over him. She shot them an embarrassed look as they got out of the car. Linda came out first—falling against the horn, which blasted—then the girls, Natasha carefully carrying the carton of cigarettes. "Whoops!" said Linda, reaching into the back seat for the bag of ironing. "Announcing our presence!" The girl was sucking on a red lollipop, and she was pregnant. She was skinny, but her stomach stuck out below her tank top as if she had a giant basketball in there.

"You looking for Ma?" she said, shouting a little over the barking. She removed the lollipop from her mouth.

"What are you, stupid, Jaycee?" said Clinton. He straightened up from the bike, a wrench in his hand. "They *know* Ma."

"Oh, jeez!" The girl clapped a hand to her cherry-red lips. She laughed like crazy. "Sorry!"

"They come every fucking week!"

Linda extended her hand to the girl. "I don't think we've met! I'm Linda Bradford!" The girl put the lollipop back in her mouth and shook Linda's hand limply, her eyes downcast. A small, private smile played on her lips.

"So, you're expecting!" Linda said brightly. "When are you due?"

Clinton turned away and went abruptly back to the bike.

"September?" said the girl.

"How wonderful!"

"I hope it's not gonna hurt," she said.

"I'd try not to worry too much. I'm sure your doctor—"

Clinton spoke up. "Oh, it'll hurt!" He chuckled. "It'll kill!"

The dogs burst through the screen door, and the big one— the shepherd cross—made a beeline for Becky.

"Oh!" said Linda. "Hmm."

Natasha's sister stood motionless, her face scrunched up and her eyes closed, as the big dog jumped on her, licking her face with a frenzied excitement. Natasha could do nothing. She was more afraid of dogs than Becky was. She clutched the carton of cigarettes to her chest till Clinton hauled the dog off. "Get outta here! Get outta here!" The dog cowered away, then looped around the yard and raced back for one more turn. Becky bent her head and put her hands to her chest as it assaulted her again.

"Nice doggy, nice doggy," Linda said. She was bending down to pet the other dog, the Chihuahua.

This time Clinton kept his hand on the big dog's collar. "What are you fucking waiting for?" he said to the girl. "Take 'em in to Ma!"

To get to the living room where Ma sat, they passed through the kitchen. The sink and counters were piled with dirty dishes, and a box of Cocoa Puffs had spilled its contents over the burners of the stove. As subtly as they could, Becky and Natasha held their T-shirts to their noses so as not to inhale the cat-piss odor straight. An orange tom was picking its way between two piles of dishes to get to the sink, where a second cat, a calico, sat licking something. The kitchen table was covered in a yellow-and-green oilcloth. Tammy was sitting at one end of it. She didn't look up when they came in.

"Hi, Tammy!" said Linda.

"Hi," Tammy said sullenly. She was a vastly overweight girl of about sixteen.

"You reading the *paper*, Tammy?" Linda asked hopefully.

"I'm doing the jumble."

"Ah, the jumble! Girls, say hello."

"Hi," the girls said.

Tammy ignored them.

"I've brought the ironing, Tammy." Linda held up the bag. "I'll leave it right here, okay? No, right... *here*. I'll leave it right here by the door and you can give it to Angie when she gets home from work."

"Okay."

Linda paused in the doorway to the living room. "Did you think about the class?" she asked. She looked searchingly around the kitchen before her eyes settled back on Tammy. "I could drive you, you know!"

Tammy didn't reply. A calico kitten rubbed itself against Natasha's and Becky's legs, mewing loudly. Becky giggled, but Natasha felt like she might be sick.

"Once a week, Tammy. Not a huge time commitment! Wednesday nights. Barb Upshaw did it, and she lost thirty pounds! You know Barb Upshaw? She lives right down the road. Ma used to work for Barb, remember? Ma took care of her twins! That was after me and before the Brennans."

Tammy looked impassively at Linda.

"All right, well, you think about it, Tammy! I'm here to help. Oh, and I'll see you tonight! Seven o'clock, yes? Do you need a ride?"

"Clinton's driving me."

"Great. Super! Thank you for doing this for me, Tammy. It's a real help."

The girl looked annoyed. "Well, you're paying me, aren't you?"

"Of course I am! Of course, Tammy. But still—it's a real help."

Tammy went back to the jumble. "Okay."

Nowadays, Ma could barely move. The sofa where she sat crocheting during the day had become her bed as well. She could no longer get upstairs. It was a combination of the obesity, the diabetes, and some condition that swelled up her legs like pontoons so that she could wear only flip-flops, not real shoes. Her feet were so swollen, they were round, as if the actual foot had been surrounded by a layer of dough, the flip-flops baked into the top.

"Well, I've brought your cigarettes, Ma," Linda said, resignation in her voice.

"Bad habit," Ma said with a girlish giggle. From deep in her face, her eyes rested on Natasha and Becky. "Look at your beautiful girls," she said as Natasha presented the carton. Her speaking voice was soft, tranquil. "God is good, isn't He, girls? Blessed Jehovah is everywhere if you look." She took the carton from Natasha and tucked it away to her side. With an effort, she shifted her weight forward. "Girls, did you know that Penelope had kittens? Did Tammy show you?"

Natasha hesitated because they *had* seen a kitten, but Tammy hadn't shown it to them.

"She didn't take you to see the kittens in the shed? Goddamn it!" Ma stopped to cough. "I told her to, Linda! I told her right before you got here. I can't do anything with that child! She's been nothing but trouble since the day she was born!"

"Now, Ma," Linda said.

"I can't trust her with a quarter, Linda!" When the girls'

mother looked unconvinced, Ma protested, "She steals money from my purse! My own daughter. Tammy!" she yelled. "Tammy, you get in here!"

"It's okay, Ma!" Linda said. "We'll see them on the way out. Now, where's Donny today? I want to ask him what he thought of that book I brought him."

"He's over at the church," Ma said. The Moores were Witnesses. It meant you couldn't say the pledge or celebrate your birthday in school—none of the kids from the hollow did. Natasha thought it also meant you couldn't go to the dentist. Instead, you went around telling people about your religion, knocking on doors. People were mean to you—they were rude to your face. They didn't want their doors knocked on. Kristin Coon said her dad had told the Witnesses to go fuck themselves.

"Actually"—Natasha spoke up when she could—"I have to go to the bathroom."

"You know where it is," Ma said gently, pointing to the stairs. She loved children and animals—that's what Linda always said. The calico kitten jumped onto the couch and Ma held it and stroked it with her plump white hands.

Natasha would take her time going, and when she returned, Becky would ask to go. The cat litter was in the upstairs bathroom so it smelled bad up there too, but still, a trip to the bathroom bought you a couple of minutes. If you ran into Donny, it wasn't quite worth it, 'cause he would want to talk and you had to be polite even when he looked so intensely at you through his thick lenses and wanted to show you one of his lizards or snakes. But he was at the church today.

*   *   *

Tammy arrived to babysit when their mother was still getting dressed. The girls were outside playing in the yard when Clinton roared up beside the house in his white pickup. Tammy got out and slammed the door, and the pregnant girl, Jaycee, slid over and took Tammy's seat by the window, giggling. "Thanks for nothing!" Tammy yelled as Clinton drove off down the road. Tammy turned toward the house, muttering, "Assholes." Her expression didn't change as she took in the girls standing beside the two pines with the hammock strung up between them. Then her eyes fixed on the corner of the house—their father's hydrangeas—and she stole forward. "Here, kitty! Here, kitty, kitty, kitty!"

Natasha and Becky stopped playing mail-order bride and watched her with a sinking feeling, hoping Clio would run away. Instead, Clio arched her black back and came forward to be stroked. Tammy snatched her up. "I got you!" She buried her face in Clio's fur. "Ah-brrr!" The cat writhed in her arms. "Ah-brrr!" Tammy said, laughing, doing it anyway. "Ha-ha-ha-ha! *Ow!*" Tammy tossed the cat away from her onto the driveway tar. "Fucking shit cat! Ow!" she said again. She sounded impressed, though, as she examined the scratch on her forearm.

"You shouldn't say that," Natasha told her. "You shouldn't swear."

"Oh, really?" Tammy said archly. "Is that so?"

"It's bad to swear."

"Who died and made you queen?" said Tammy, but, as with the scratch, she was good-humored about it.

Their mother and father emerged from the house. They were dressed up. It was a cocktail party over at the Brennans'. Linda was in fuchsia—a long bright cotton dress with drapey sleeves. She wore beads around her neck and leather sandals, and her dark blond hair was in two braids that she had pinned up, Scandinavian-style. Their father was freshly shaven in a dark suit. He jiggled the keys walking to the car. He didn't notice the cat skulking off. He wasn't an animal person. You couldn't tell him anything about the cat.

"Tammy!" exclaimed Linda, as if she were surprised to see her. "I'm so glad you could come."

Tammy looked sheepish and glanced over at their father.

"I've left some sugar-free wheat-germ cake for dessert. They can watch *The Muppet Show.*" She came over to kiss the girls goodbye. Neither Natasha nor Becky said a word or moved to embrace her. She was an utter irrelevance at this point. They watched their father get into the Buick. So did Tammy. Linda got in, and their father started the car and drove off, their mother waving out the window until the car turned the corner: "Bye! Have fun! We'll be back before you know it!"

"Jesus!" Tammy said disgustedly. "It's only for the night!"

She trudged over and lay down on the hammock. She was so heavy, it sank nearly to the ground. "Pretend I'm a mean rich lady and you girls have to wait on me. I'm a real bitch!" She made them bring her sticks and rocks—Natasha added bunches of pine needles. "Make me a white Russian! No, make me a Kahlúa and cream! Make it a double!" Tammy said, lying sunken in the hammock, looking up at the trees. She closed her eyes for a moment. When she opened them, she strained to sit up but couldn't, so she rolled herself out of the hammock and onto the ground. As she was pushing herself to sit, she leered at them and said, "Your father's a lot older than your mother."

"So?" said Natasha.

"He's, like, old enough to be her father."

"He was in World War Two," Becky said.

"Shut up!" Tammy cried. "There's no way."

"He was."

"Liar."

"We have his uniform."

"Liar, liar, pants on fire."

"My sister doesn't lie."

Tammy made a face. "'My sister doesn't lie.' How would you even know?"

"I know."

"Can we watch *The Muppet Show*?" Becky said.

While the girls watched TV, sitting together in the big chair, Tammy looked around the kitchen, opening cabinets. They could hear her in there, squawking when something she saw surprised or tickled her. It was the same as last time. The difference was that last time, their parents had been across the street, at the Trainors', for Mr. Trainor's retirement party. The Brennans lived all the way across town, close to the elementary school. The Brennan girls were walkers.

During a commercial, Tammy appeared, holding a glass of something. "Your parents have some weird shit in the liquor cabinet," she said. "They don't have Kahlúa, though. I know a ton of drinks with Kahlúa." She took a sip of the drink she was holding. "Here, smell this." She waved the glass under the girls' noses.

"Ew." Natasha wrinkled up her face.

"Licorice, right? Can you smell it?" Tammy knocked back the rest of the glass and looked at the TV. She said suddenly, as if she had just noticed, "You only have black-and-white?" She sounded outraged. "Can't you afford color?"

"Our mom doesn't believe in television," said Natasha.

Tammy looked incensed. "That's fucking retarded!"

"No, it's not."

"Yuh-huh. It's not something you believe in. It just *is*." She laughed. "What does she think, it's God?"

"Too much TV is bad for you," Natasha said levelly, her eyes on the screen.

"Oh, really? You don't say."

"You should be reading books."

"You don't say!" Although Tammy's expression still registered scorn, there was some humor in it too. She watched the program for a couple of minutes, looking rapt. Her face softened. "Ha-ha—I love that one. I love the big bird. He's so fucking funny."

"It's not Big Bird," Natasha said. "That's *Sesame Street*."

"I didn't fuckin' *say* it was Big Bird! I said *the* big bird. Jesus H. Christ! Wicked fucking brat, aren't you?"

"His name is Sam," said Becky.

"Can we watch *Dukes of Hazzard*?" Natasha asked. Becky glanced up at Tammy too.

She looked at them incredulously. Then she shook her head as if she just gave up. "Sure, kids, watch whatever the hell you want."

They watched *Dukes of Hazzard*. Tammy went up the back stairs. They heard her traipsing around in the room above the television, their parents' room. "Oh, shit!" they heard. Then it was silent for a while. Eventually, Tammy came back down—only it didn't sound like Tammy. They heard a careful, halting movement on the stairs, not like Tammy's usual kick-slam-flop rhythm. She appeared in the doorway. Somehow, she had gotten a pink silk evening gown over her head and onto her torso. The skirt of the gown was bunched up at her waist. She was wearing silver high heels and had a fur stole around her shoulders. She had put heavy lipstick on, and she hadn't managed to color inside the lines—clownishly, it spread out onto the skin around her lips too. "How do I look?" She grabbed bunches of the gown in both hands and teetered around on the silver high heels. The gown was unzipped, stretched taut across her back in an open V.

"She never wears that anyway," Natasha said coldly.

"Who, your mother? Why not?"

"The fur is Grammy's," said Becky.

"No, it's not!" Natasha snapped. "It was Grandma Jane's. She's dead," she added.

"You know how they make these, right?" Tammy said, swiveling her shoulders and trying to look at her reflection in the dark window.

"Yes," said Natasha. "We know."

"We know," Becky echoed.

"They raise these cute little, cute little minxes…and then, *bam!* They electrocute them."

"We *know*," said Natasha. "We already knew that." In fact, she'd thought minks were wild animals that men shot. Now she knew.

On the TV, the sheriff's car ran smack into a hay wagon. The two girls giggled.

Tammy said, "You want me to tell you something?"

Becky looked at her sister. Natasha lifted her shoulders in a shrug.

"The last time Penelope had kittens, Ma made Clinton drown them in the pond."

Natasha shrugged again.

"You could hear them mewing as they went down. Something else? When Ma was watching Angie's baby, it was her fault Ricky got burned. She was trying to teach him a lesson. I'm not allowed to tell or she won't get any more money for the foster kids."

All three of them heard the knock on the door—a knocking so faint, at first they all thought perhaps it was just the wind. But then they heard it again.

"You have to answer it!" Tammy looked scared as she pointed at Natasha. "I can't go like this!"

"I'll go!" Becky shot out of the chair and into the hallway. Natasha and Tammy looked at each other. They heard Becky opening the door and talking to someone.

"Who is it?" Natasha called to her.

There was a pause, then Becky said, "I don't remember!"

Natasha and Tammy raised their eyebrows at each other. "What's their name?" Natasha called back, giggling a little.

Another pause, then: "Jaycee!"

"Jaycee? Fucking kidding me!" Tammy picked up her skirts and went down the hall to the door. Natasha trailed after her.

The front door was wide open, letting in all the bugs that swarmed around the outdoor light, and Clinton's pregnant girlfriend was standing there with her face screwed up, as if she were afraid Tammy would strike her. She put up her hands. "I'm sorry, Tammy!" She hadn't made a move to come inside. "Don't be mad at me!"

"What the hell are you doing here?" said Tammy.

Jaycee took in Tammy's outfit and snorted.

"Don't you say nothing!" Tammy pumped a fist at her. "Why the fuck are you here? Ain't I working?"

"Close the door! The bugs!" said Natasha, doing it herself.

Jaycee stepped into the hallway. "Clinton got pissed at me— he dropped me down the road." She looked at the girls. "Thought these two would be in bed, Tammy."

"They're going to bed!" Tammy shouted. "I'm in charge here, Jaycee!"

With one hand cradling her basketball, Jaycee got awkwardly down to her knees. She stretched out her arm. "What's the cat called? Here, kitty, kitty. Here, kitty!"

"Don't you touch the cat!" Tammy ordered. "I'm in charge, Jaycee!"

"I know you are, Tammy! I know you are!" Jaycee raised her eyes, coquettish and pleading. "Please, Tammy? It's too far to Ma's. I can't walk all the way, not like this." She looked down the Bradfords' hall, its walls covered in family photographs, toward the open door, and her expression seemed to quicken. "Can I help you? I could help you." She appealed to Natasha and Becky. "Girls, I know how to French-braid. I could French-braid your hair."

Natasha's hand went to her hair but her expression remained unpersuaded, and she glanced at Tammy.

"You're not braiding anything," Tammy said, but the response seemed to come belatedly, as if she couldn't quite keep up. She reminded Natasha of a boy in school, a kid who took forever doing his times tables but wouldn't let anyone help him.

"Okay, fine, fine. How 'bout we watch TV? What are you girls watching?"

"*Dallas* is on?" Natasha suggested.

"I have to change," Tammy said stiffly.

"Ooh, I love *Dallas*! Sue Ellen is so mean! Don't you just hate her?" Jaycee looked at Natasha. "Help me up, honey?" Natasha helped her to her feet, the basketball forcing Jaycee to brace herself at odd angles. "You go change, Tammy. Come on, honey," she said, holding out her other hand to Becky. "Let's go watch *Dallas*! You go change, Tam! I got this! You girls have a wicked nice house here, you know that?"

She didn't watch TV with them. She sat on the edge of the sofa ripping at her nails and after a minute, she said, "Don't move, girls. I'll be right back. I have to go ask Tammy something! But when I come back, I'll braid your hair, okay?" Natasha didn't even bother to nod. Jaycee was one of those types. She was like the older Brennan girl, the one who'd said she'd pay them a dollar if they prank-called a friend of hers but, after Natasha did it, never gave her the dollar. Nothing that came out of the mouths of people like that was factual.

During a commercial break, Tammy came down and went into the kitchen. She clinked around in there, singing under her breath. Natasha left Becky nodding off in the big chair. She went and stood silently in the kitchen doorway. Tammy had their mother's big green jug of wine in her hands and she was holding it up and peering at it. She looked funny because despite having changed back into her shorts and T-shirt, she still had all the makeup on her face and was still wearing the silver high heels.

"What are you doing?"

"Jesus!" Tammy jumped and clutched at the jug. "You scared the shit outta me! Jesus! Never you mind!" she said sternly. "Hey!" She shook a finger at Natasha. "You're supposed to be in bed!"

"You said we could watch—"

"I don't care what I said! You gotta go to bed!"

Natasha turned and ran back to the TV room. She stood at the threshold listening for a second, but Tammy did not come after her. Becky had fallen asleep in the big chair. Natasha squeezed in beside her. From time to time she would get up, turn the volume down on the television, go out of the room, and listen at the back stairs. She heard Tammy going up and down them a couple of times and her and Jaycee laughing and carrying on. At one point the telephone upstairs crashed to the floor.

"We're fine!" Jaycee yelled. "We're fine!"

Natasha rubbed her eyes and tried to stay awake, but she must have nodded off too, because suddenly she heard a fight going on and she had no idea how it had started, and the TV was playing something she didn't recognize—it was that late.

"Take it off!" she heard Tammy shout. "Take it off!" Heavy footsteps pounded on the ceiling above.

Natasha listened as the fight got louder and louder. She started going through her times tables, saying them in a whisper, all the way through the elevens. The girls were now screaming at each other. Natasha went out to the hallway and looked up the stairs in time to see Jaycee appear at the top.

She was wearing their father's dress blue uniform and carrying his hat. "How do I look?" she said, batting her eyes. She placed the hat on her head at a rakish angle. The jacket looked like a disfigured person—it was stretched taut across her middle, only one button buttoned, but the shoulders were enormous and the sleeves hung down over her hands. Her feet were buried in the long pants legs. She spied Natasha and saluted, sticking her tongue out the side of her mouth and making a face. "Colonel Klink, reporting for duty!"

Tammy loomed behind her. Her eyes met Natasha's, and she looked frightened. "Gimme that!" she hollered, swiping broadly at the hat. "Gimme the fucking hat!" She lunged for it again, but Jaycee shrank back. Tammy stumbled—horribly— but managed to seize the banister, hold on, and wrench herself back up. "Holy fuck! I almost fell!" There was a beat, then Jaycee began to laugh, her eyes enormous. "Oh my fucking God, oh my fucking God."

As if inspired by Jaycee's distraction, Tammy made another lunge for the hat, but even pregnant, Jaycee was quicker, flattening herself against the stairway wall. Pitching forward at the top of the steps, Tammy swatted at nothing.

Natasha felt as if she had never actually caught her breath before. She made a sound like in a movie, the sharp involuntary intake of air. From where she was standing, Tammy looked like a bad diver as she came down, like one of those kids you saw at the town pool who'd never been properly taught. They would end up doing belly-flops. There was a crack, then an enormous thud as she slammed down onto the floor. *Poor Tammy! Poor Tammy!* she thought. It was their father who had seen to their swimming and diving—there were no arm floaties; no training wheels when you learned to ride a bike. "We don't believe in that crap," Natasha said to herself.

"Shit," Tammy said. Her voice was cracked-muffled, as if it came from deep inside her. "Shit—I can't move." Her head, on the wooden floor, was turned away from her body. Becky slept like that, on her stomach with her head turned to the side. The silver straps looked painfully tight around her feet. Then, at the top of the stairs, Jaycee began to scream. Still flattening herself against the wall, she screamed and screamed and screamed and screamed. Occasionally her eyes would meet Natasha's and she would look away again, as if she were frightened by the sight of her. Natasha didn't know her sister was behind her till she sensed movement and turned and saw her standing there. "I woke up," Becky said. She looked sleepy and rubbed her eyes.

When the girls' parents got home, they saw Clinton's white pickup truck parked on the side of the road. Becky appeared in the doorway so promptly, it was as if she had been standing watch. "Don't worry!" she cried, sounding pleased, as well she might; she had been waiting a long time to be the one to tell them. "Tashie called 911!" She waved her arms and jumped up and down, trying to make her parents understand that it was all under control—the ambulance had already come and gone. "Tashie called for help!"

Residents Only

In February, the week before we were to leave for Acapulco, Vero called to say she was not going to make it.

Of course, I could still use the condo. It was all arranged—arranged so perfectly, in fact, that I wondered if Vero had ever really been planning to come. Her aunt's maid would come in every day and would cook lunch too. "Wait till you try her *rajas con crema!* And her tamales! You'll be in heaven!" I had always admired the way Vero could tell someone no so cheerfully that the person ended up apologizing to *her*—even thanking her, as I did, for the slap in the face. The key to it I think was her forthrightness; she didn't squirm or condescend in order to mitigate the letdown: "I'm so sorry to have to tell you and I wish things were different, but..." No, she just put it out there: "I won't be coming!" That ease she had in setting boundaries, that joyful frankness that was a hallmark of her character, I attributed to her having grown up as a member of the elite in

a country where it was abundantly clear who belonged to it—
that is to say, an inherited elite that clung both tenaciously and
effortlessly to its position.

I have a part-time housekeeper, Estelita. She herself is Mexican,
so she was on my mind as we flew south, though I recognized
that thinking of one's cleaner on this type of trip was solipsistic
in the extreme, the kind of connection made only by a stay-
at-home mom whose help took up far too much of her mental
space. Nevertheless, I fervently wished I could conjure her up
when, after a long and exhausting day of travel, the girls and
I finally made it to Playa Mar. My husband's family owns a
beach house on the Rhode Island shore. We always have the
first half of the summer—Cal's brother takes the second—so
it falls to us to open up the house for the season. For the past
few years, since my younger daughter, Genie, was born, we'd
taken to bringing Estelita with us that first weekend to organize
the kitchen and help us unpack. The calm, unhurried way she
works reminds me of that passage in Tolstoy when Dolly has to
open up the dacha for the summer—Estelita, too, could have
found a cow to milk if I'd needed her to, could have whipped
up dinner out of dirt and air. Without her, I was alone on
a third-floor walkway in the tropical February darkness with
two little girls and our shockingly heavy bags—one enormous
clothes suitcase and the girls' small one, jammed with coloring books and stuffed animals—trying to figure out, with an
increasing sense of panic, why the code Vero had given me
wouldn't open the door to the apartment.

"Are we locked out?" Celia, my older one, who was seven,
said in the suspicious tone she used when she asked me,

"What's for dinner?" on Estelita's days off. "We're locked out, aren't we?" A sudden gust from the ocean rustled the trees below, and I laughed so as not to show I was trembling. The first night in the tropics is a bit frightening, I find. It takes a day or two to shake off the feeling that you have done something wrong—that the ease with which you exchanged filthy streets of slush and mounds of trash-strewn ice for hot sand, warm breezes, and the smell of honeysuckle is akin to committing a crime and that punishments will ensue, even if they are dilatory and not obvious.

We had a three-hour layover in Mexico City. I had nodded off, again and again, my head drooping uncontrollably toward my chest. Both girls, even little Genie, found it hilarious that I simply could not keep my eyes open no matter how hard I tried. I suppose they see me as always in control, and it was funny to them that Mom was helpless in the face of her own exhaustion. I had been up packing most of the night before. Packing and also making a point—the point I seemed destined to make over and over in my marriage: that I was not, appearances to the contrary, dependent on Cal. I was one of those tough independent-minded mothers who take their girls on their promised holidays even when their flaky friends cancel. Despite the fact that Vero and I had planned it as a girls' trip—she and I, her two, and my two; "the girl party," she had christened it—I was no fool. Even months before, when I hinted about Mexico to her, explaining that Cal's work was so nuts he wouldn't be able to get away at all this winter and that we'd already made the obligatory pilgrimage to Disney World, and Vero had said readily, "We'll go to my aunt's condo in Acapulco!" I knew there was a fifty-fifty chance she wouldn't make it. I met Vero in college. From the way she approached, say, what classes to take—with an air of mild, detached curiosity, while the rest of us agonized over our majors, the number of credits we needed, and of course our grades—we, her roommates, came to understand that we were American grinds without an original idea in our heads, and Vero was not. College wasn't particularly important to Verónica Escalante. She would come back to the dorm with a bouquet of deli tulips and say, "I have just bought the most beautiful flowers in a shop on Elm Street!" in the same tone we would use to say we'd made the first cut for the Rhodes. Nothing, ultimately, was all that important to Vero. Perhaps nothing ever was when you were a member of an established elite. So when she did, ultimately, bail on the girl party, I could hardly pose as indignant. I half hoped Cal would stop me from going alone—or would at least voice concern—but that wasn't Cal. Our entire young marriage, it seemed, I'd been announcing, "I've bought my crampons for the Kilimanjaro ascent," and he'd been responding, hardly looking up from his work, "Okay, let me know your dates when you get a sec." That night, as I stuffed bathing suits into side pockets and counted our passports, I swore I wouldn't call him if anything went wrong—and I never did.

When I travel in a developing country, I can't bear to be confined to a tourists' bunker. It makes me insane to be trapped on the gated grounds of Whitey's hotel. I become distractingly claustrophobic no matter how many acres the resort "boasts," as the travel websites say, or how many amenities it offers. Any time Cal and I travel together, it is a point not only of pride, though there is that too, but of pleasure that we always leave the hotel and go into the town, however small and insignificant or big, crazy, "scary," and overwhelming it is. I am proud to say that, on the very first day in Acapulco, I hired a taxi to take us from the aunt's condominium complex to a cove Vero had described where we could rent a boat. *I* got us there; *I* hired a *lancha* and driver to take us on a tour of the harbor. My high-school Spanish served me well. I was able to do the negotiating myself. I even insisted on life jackets for the girls, but that turned out to be a given. It was spectacular on the boat—to see Acapulco from the bay—the azure water stretching away, the houses and hotels stacked like jewels encrusted onto the mountain beyond. Even the air seemed to glow with the retro glamour of JFK and Jackie and Frank Sinatra. I began to hum "Come Fly with Me," which Cal and I had danced to at our wedding, and to teach the girls the words. I held Genie on my lap, and the boat's driver, Miguel, let Celia sit up next to him. When we went home at the end of the week and Cal asked me what the highlight of the trip was, I didn't hesitate. "Going out on the boat in Acapulco Bay," I said, "on the very first day." I told him nothing of what had happened at the end of the boat ride. And of course I never told him the rest. There are some things that can make even your husband see you differently. You have to protect him more than you do your children from your foolishness and mental frailty.

When the boat ride was ending and we drew near the cove, Miguel killed the motor, hopped out of the launch into the shallow water of the bay, and tugged the boat toward the sand. Despite the setting sun, it was still hot out. Celia wanted to jump into the water too, so I let her, and then Genie wanted to follow, though it was up to her waist. I got out with her and kept hold of her hand. I had to keep hauling her up, straight-armed, when she lost her footing. Splashing and chatting, our party approached the beach, until all at once, Miguel stopped the boat with his hand on the bow. He made a motion to indicate we should fall in behind him. At the top of the beach, two men were having an altercation with the man who'd rented me the boat—this was a different person than Miguel, who had waited down by the boats until I paid the money.

My city had been so safe, so malled over for so many years now, thanks to people like Cal and me colonizing it after college with our exacting coffee demands and our big-box stores and chain pharmacies, that I hadn't had that feeling in more than a decade—the feeling of going from blithe distraction to the most acutely paralyzing fear in a matter of seconds. The two men on the beach were dressed in street clothes and shoes. They began to rough up the proprietor of the boat-rental shack. They went about it good-naturedly. They wore grins as they pushed him, slapped his face back and forth. He himself was arguing—shouting and throwing his hands up. He wasn't taking it lying down, as they say. I grabbed Genie and clutched her to my chest; I turned Celia's face into my abdomen. I kept my focus down—on the top of my daughter's head, on the water. I simply couldn't believe this was happening. When I dared to glance up the beach, they had pushed the proprietor down to the sand. One of the attackers laughed and gave him a vicious kick in the ribs. "Ay!" the man cried out. He rolled to his side. The other man brandished a gun, and at that very moment, he turned in our direction and his eyes scanned the water. I thought for an instant that they'd met mine, but perhaps he was only looking past us, to the horizon. The blood pounded in my temples. He turned away and shot into the air. Someone screamed. My children gripped me tighter. There was a handmade little bar down the way, just a hut and a few tables. A couple sitting at one of the tables jumped up and ran down the beach into the water. The girls and I cowered in our huddle. Then it was over. With another glance around, the men jogged quickly away. They disappeared behind the shack. A few seconds later, a car drove off. Miguel dropped the bowline and ran up the sand. The girls and I guided the boat to shore as he got the proprietor to his feet. The man howled out his complaints, shaking a finger in the air. Miguel helped him limp to the shack.

The whole way back in the taxi to Playa Mar, I felt as if I'd been awakened from a dream. The reality of the situation was brought home to me; only now could I look at things squarely. With a sinking feeling, I realized I would not leave the condominium complex again—that I never should have left it in the first place, that it had been a vain, bullheaded thing to do. I had known that the area wasn't completely safe. "Actually, before you go, let me ask my aunt. There've been a couple of incidents lately…" Vero had said, but I never followed up. A Google search when I planned the trip warned of increased crime in surrounding neighborhoods. I had known, but I cared more about proving something to myself. In order to distinguish myself from the weak, cowed American mother in my head, I had put all of our lives at risk. It was only in hindsight a few years after the trip that I could see that it wasn't only vanity that drove me. The truth was, when my children were small, I was driven half insane by the mental and emotional demands they made. When I look back at that time, I realize that I was always trying to escape. There were other poor, impulsive decisions I made—shortcuts I took when I was at the end of my rope. Sometimes I am surprised I made it through.

We had no Estelita in Acapulco; we had Reyna. She arrived in the midmorning the day after we did. The night before, when I hadn't been able to get the door code to work, we'd had to trudge back downstairs. I left the suitcases on the landing, took the girls with me, and went to ask the gatehouse security guard, who controlled the entrance to the condominiums, to let us into the condo. He had waved my taxi from the airport through twenty minutes before—surely he would understand. When we got back down there, though—crossing the large, empty flagstone terrace that surrounded the pool, skirting the deserted cocktail bar, walking the hundred yards or so along the gravel path from the condominiums to the parking lot and from there along the asphalt to the gatehouse—that affable man with his ready smile was nowhere to be seen. He had been replaced by a younger man in military dress whose expression was discouragingly blank.

We spoke in Spanish.

"No, but I'm supposed to be here, you see."

"But you say you do not know the code, madam."

"No, I *know* it, I *know* it—my friend gave it to me! It's just not *working*."

"Your friend, madam?" I had said "my sister" initially, afraid that I would get Vero in trouble with her aunt. She had told Tía Mercedes, of course, that I was coming, but the rules of the tenants' association, she said, didn't allow for nonrelatives to come alone. "They'll think she's renting it!" my friend had explained in the tone you might use to say, "They'll think she's running a prostitution ring out of the apartment!"

"Well, it's actually—a friend, you know, a sister." I tried to smile, appalled by the guilt I seemed to be projecting. Of course I had been robo-dialing Vero nonstop—after spending twenty minutes on the balcony with AT&T trying to sort out an international data plan—but her number kept going straight to voice mail. The guard ushered me inside and offered me his landline so I could call "the owner." I simply had to get into the condo and I realized I had no choice but to dial Tía Mercedes in Mexico City and explain everything. But when he showed me the contact on his laminated list of tenants, the owner of 33F was listed as one V. Escudero with an address in the United States. When I hesitated, the guard took a call on his phone, looking at me the whole time, then nodded briefly, hung up, and demanded to see our passports.

"Are you kidding?" I said in English. He was not.

After searching my purse—sitting outside on the steps of the gatehouse underneath the harsh beam of the searchlight and dumping all of the contents out of it—I remembered I had left them upstairs in my carry-on. It was only after I toiled back upstairs to get them, half dragging, half carrying the girls, that Vero's number suddenly popped up on my phone. She was laughing, apologizing: "I am at dinner and I turned my ringer off!" After some back-and-forth, during which I insisted I had typed in the code correctly (but dreaded the possibility that I had not), Vero screamed. She realized she'd given me the wrong code. At this moment, the door two units down opened and a poker-faced old woman stuck her head out. I waggled my fingers and mouthed, *So sorry!* She did not react visibly to this, and when I tried again to appeal to her sympathy, rolling my eyes to indicate the ineptitude of the person on the other end of the phone, she quickly closed the door.

"You see—it wasn't my fault!" I said testily afterward to Celia, who had expressed her typically dim view of my competence. *Damn it, Vero!* I thought. It was so her—strong on enthusiasm, weak on detail. She laughed like mad when she said, "Oh my God, I gave you the code for my own garage!" She stayed on the phone with me as we pushed the door to the condo open and felt for the light switch. I walked through the apartment, unlocked the sliding glass doors, and stepped out onto the balcony. I now understood the layout of the place: the three condo buildings were arranged in a horseshoe around the pool, with the bar off to one side and the sea beyond the long terrace. "It looks great," I said, going back in—relieved. Vero reminded me one more time about the pool—"No outsiders, okay? Don't bring anyone in. They are snobs of the first water. You think you have seen snobs? You have no idea." I hung up wondering exactly what outsiders she thought I would be inviting over to swim, but in retrospect I think she was just using the pool as an excuse to warn me about the other tenants—not to expect it to be like home.

Reyna came from up in the hills and took an hour-long bus ride each way to work for Tía Mercedes. Her mother owned (or cooked at?) a restaurant (or more of a pop-up lunch stand?) up where she came from, and that was where she had learned to cook. Vero had not exaggerated the woman's culinary skills. Every dish she made tasted like an expression of authenticity, but the authenticity itself was elusive. You could never say what

Reyna did differently than a Mexican restaurant at home. At first I asked and asked: What spice is that? How do you skin the peppers? Do you do that in the blender? Now that I didn't dare leave Playa Mar, I had so much time to kill. I loitered in the kitchen when Reyna buttoned on her uniform. I spoke to her in half-hour jags. I was giddy—overfriendly. I might have seemed hysterical.

In the next few days, the girls and I traipsed from the third-floor apartment to the beach to Reyna's lunch table on the apartment terrace. The vacation took on an emotional rhythm. I felt optimistic on the beach in the mornings, anxious and glum as the day wore on, and I overate at lunch, as if to combat the claustrophobia. Celia loved the tamales; Genie was ruined for real food by the smoothies Reyna made for them in the blender with fresh papayas. The lunches were enormous and filled me with anxiety. Reyna would spend the morning shut up in the kitchen cooking half a dozen dishes. After a couple of days of this, I tried to talk her out of putting on such an elaborate spread. I couldn't condone the waste; as the one adult, I tried to stanch it by overeating. She was good-humored when I spoke to her about it, but it had no effect whatever. "At least take it home," I'd beg and then I'd have to absent myself from the kitchen in case it actually ended up in the trash.

Late afternoons we spent at the condominium's pool. There was never anyone else there. Hardly anyone was staying at the place, period—I was lucky if I passed three people in a day, and those I did pass would never speak to or even so much as acknowledge me. I had quickly stopped saying hello when my greetings were met with frowns. But the pool was as deserted as if we had climbed a fence and sneaked into a hotel off-season.

The sign was there, as Vero had warned me it would be. A little white wooden sign on a stake in the grass: RESIDENTS ONLY, it read in script—in English. Though we had our pick of two tiers of a dozen chairs on each side of the pool, we stuck to sharing one or two in a corner by the shallow end. On the first day, I got up three times and reread the rules posted on the side of the little pool house/bathroom. Had I, perhaps, confused the hours that the pool was open? The sign said 07:00 to 22:00. I recalculated twice, but no, 22:00 was 10:00 p.m. The three condo buildings that made up the horseshoe had uniform window shades of dark green. Every time I walked from my chair to read the rules, I felt as if I were being watched from behind the shades by phantom people who never came out of their apartments. I smiled and tried to look confident, called lightly to the girls who were testing the water from the stairs in the shallow end. When I realized I'd made a mistake by bringing towels from the condo, I said loudly, "Oh, look, there *are* pool towels! Now we know"—as if someone could hear me.

My isolation was compounded by the fact that I wasn't supposed to be there. Once or twice from my chaise longue, I noticed two men having a drink over at the bar. I was desperate enough that I might have walked toward them and made an overture, but I am a rule-follower—perhaps that is as American as our tone deafness, our expectation of niceness back if we are nice—and I didn't know what I would say. The hours inched by. I grew more and more restless on my chair, but though the girls begged me, I couldn't seem to make myself swim. It was as if I had to keep my guard up and could not do two things at once. Toward the end of the afternoon, I would get in and stand anxiously in the shallow end, running my hands through the warm water. One afternoon, standing there, I saw a uniformed maid leaning on the railing of one of the second-floor balconies, but when I smiled up at her, she went quickly inside and closed the door. At night, after the girls were asleep, I watched a Vegas-style variety show on TV and got drunk on a dusty bottle of tequila I had ferreted out of a liquor cabinet so neglected, I wondered if Tía Mercedes even remembered it was there—its door had stuck mightily and I'd had to pry it open with a knife. I would have liked to buy my own alcohol so I didn't have to mete it out, but I didn't know how. Reyna showed up in the mornings laden with plastic bags of groceries, but I shied away from asking her to buy booze, feeling as if the request would expose me somehow. I had never met Tía Mercedes, but I didn't want her to know I drank alone.

One afternoon in the middle of the week when the girls and I went out to the pool, another woman was there. By this point, I had adopted a "Whistle a Happy Tune" mode in the public spaces and was chatting away to the girls when I saw her. She was a slim, well-preserved silvery blonde in sunglasses and a black-and-gold bikini. She lay opposite our chairs, close to the diving board, reading a novel. Sitting down carefully and taking my things out, I realized I had seen her once or twice in passing—walking on the beach, then having a drink at the poolside bar, conversing with the bartender. The girls had elicited a promise from me to go in the pool with them that day, so after blowing up Genie's arm floaties, I got in and, feeling silly, joined their game. It was a sort of pool version of telephone that Celia had invented—one of us said something underwater and the other two tried to translate it above the water. I glanced over at the woman once or twice, but she was ignoring us— pointedly, I felt. I became increasingly self-conscious about the game and the noise we were making. As soon as I could, I got out and lay down on a chair myself. Celia and Genie continued the game. To my dismay, they were being louder than usual. After an initial period of shyness and quietude, my girls realized there were no other children at the resort to cow them into servility. When they yelled particularly loudly, I sat up and said brightly, for the benefit of the other woman, "Oh, dear! They may have heard that in Miami!" The woman's sunglasses had those opaque blue reflective lenses. I sensed that from where she lay on the chaise longue, she was looking at me from behind them...and that she was cutting me dead.

Somewhat pathetically, my eyes smarted. But then I got annoyed. What kind of a place didn't expect children to make noise in a pool? The average age of the residents at the condo made me feel even more of an anomaly. Vero might have warned me that, as the only person with children, I'd stick out a mile. With her, I would have enjoyed the safety in numbers; alone, I was a spectacle. At that point, Celia shouted at Genie, and Genie got out of the pool and ran over to me, crying. The silvery-blond woman slipped a dark dress over her bikini and left the pool, her face wrinkled up into a look I associate with constipation in children. Soon she was having a drink at the bar with the two men I had seen. I snapped at the girls. "Pool time over!"

When we got upstairs, my heart started to pound. The young, blank-faced security guard from the other day was standing outside 33F and banging on the door.

158

"Excuse me!" I said. "Excuse me! Is there something you need?"

"I need your passports, madam. You never returned with them."

"What are you talking about?" I said rudely. "It's not a hotel." Nevertheless, he insisted—in Spanish. I had the feeling he was purposely speaking quickly and using complicated vocabulary so that I couldn't fully understand the explanation. I heard the door a couple of units down open as it had the previous time, but when I turned to glare at the woman—I was done trying to make nice—it closed again just as quickly. "Fuck you," I muttered under my breath. I went inside and found the passports in my purse and handed them over. As luck would have it, Reyna, who was usually meticulous, had missed the bottle of tequila—it stood uncapped on top of the television cabinet, where I'd left it the night before, right beside my handbag. When the guard left, I went to put it away, thought better of it, and had a swig from the bottle. Then I got a glass and poured myself a drink.

All night I tossed and turned. That truculent, protective type of fear gripped me, the kind you feel when a plane is boarding and, for now, you have the adjoining seat to yourself. "I've done nothing wrong!" I said aloud a couple of times. And "Fuck them! Fuck them all."

The next morning was the first cloudy day we'd had—not much of a beach day. If anything, it was a pool day, but I didn't feel like hurrying right back out there. I let the girls laze around in their nighties until Reyna arrived around ten. This morning, along with the groceries, she had brought a young boy—her grandson. "How great!" I said, though it felt like the last straw.

Gesticulating and overenunciating, we finally understood each other: Tino was exactly the same age as Celia, seven, and Reyna hoped it was okay that she had brought him—her daughter was working. "Oh, of course, are you kidding?" I said, talking too much to cover my irritation. I announced we were going to the beach after all and hurried the girls out, wondering what the boy would do all day. I felt guilty, and then I felt resentful, sitting on my towel, watching my girls lugging sand over to build their daily sand city. That the kid's mother was working today was too bad, but it had nothing to do with me. All I wanted was to get out of here and go home. I wanted it so badly, I felt I couldn't stand it. I raised my eyes to the overcast sky. Three more days, I told myself. Our flight left Sunday afternoon. I counted the hours, the meals, the number of showers I had left to take before we got on the plane. When we returned for the late lunch that had become our habit, Reyna was gone. Normally she left at five. She had said nothing to me about leaving early—but then, I wasn't her employer. The girls and I cleaned up after lunch ourselves, in a perfunctory way. I felt helpless in my irritation. I hadn't wanted the six dishes and I didn't want the cleanup either. My girls got out their coloring books and lay on the floor with their crayons, absorbed in their coloring, and again I felt guilty and disgusted with myself. I decided to max out Reyna's tip at the end of the week. I had already been planning to, but perhaps I'd add a little more on top and say, "Buy something for your grandson."

The next day, she didn't apologize for leaving early or make any mention of it at all, but she again had the boy in tow. My heart sank when I saw him settling in to watch television, the remote already in his hand, as I counted beach towels. It was an expression of annoyance more than anything else when I said to Reyna, in Spanish, "Does Tino want to come with us to the beach today?"

"No." I was taken aback when she shook her head. *"Tiene miedo de las olas."* He's afraid of the beach—no, not the beach, the waves. He prefers the pool, I was given to understand. "Can you take him with you to the pool?" she asked frankly.

"The pool? Of course!" Then I put the heel of my hand to my head and said, "Oh, jeez, I wish I could, but they're so strict." This last bit I said in English. I wanted to convey the tone of reluctance—the impossibility of the request. I laughed and grimaced. "They don't even want *me* in the pool! There's a sign—" I pictured the RESIDENTS ONLY sign, and it seemed to me that the silvery-blond woman in the sunglasses had painted the letters and pounded it into the grass herself. I stalled, waiting for Reyna to tell me to forget it, waiting for her to let me off the hook. But she waited too, looking expectant and not at all uncomfortable. I felt a buzzing in my head similar to what I had felt when I announced to Cal, "I'm taking the girls to Acapulco by myself!"

"You know what? Screw it!" I said aloud. To Reyna, I said in Spanish, "Yes. Yes, I will take Tino to the pool." Screw these haute Mexican snobs. What sort of an example was I setting for my girls? It was just the shrinking Goody Two-shoes in me that wanted to hide behind the excuse of the sign. I had to show them that their mother was someone who lived the values she professed: I would not be snobbed into servility.

Down to the pool I went. I set myself up in the chaise longue as always but raised the back to the straightest setting so I could keep an eye on the three of them—well, on Tino, really. It occurred to me only then that I ought to have inquired as to the boy's swimming ability. Because of all the rules and my self-consciousness about the other guests, I had been putting Genie in arm floaties even though both Cal and I regarded them as suburban and lame. She fought me—had even cried—but I wasn't taking any chances. I paused in the middle of blowing them up and called to the kid, "Hey! Maybe you ought to wear these!" I pointed. "I have an extra pair." He grinned and shook me off. Little imp. Dully compliant inside the apartment, the moment the boy was away from his grandmother, a whole other personality emerged. A personality that ignored my calls of caution, raced down to the deep end of the pool, and jumped in. He surfaced immediately—and I could breathe again. But there was something about the way the boy swam that made me nervous. He seemed to have to work harder than my girls to keep his head and upper body above the water, as if he lacked the floating fallback that underlies the forward motion. He would thrash and sink a bit and come battling up, his arms churning. When he got to the shallow end, he cried something in Spanish and laughed. It sounded like "Yippee!"

"Hey!" I said sharply. "Be careful, okay? *Cuidado*, Tino!" I watched him jump in and hatchet his way down to my end again. Despite my misgivings, I felt a rush of joy that we had taken him with us. Yes, it was a distraction from the oppressive silence. But I was also just plain happy for the kid. He started playing a game where he sat on the floor of the pool and then came jumping up clapping his hands. He was grinning, shrieking—marvelously entertained by his own antics. You could tell he was a quick study. I started having a fantasy about spiriting him away with us to New York, where Celia's grade school would delight in giving him a full scholarship. I got distracted smearing sunscreen on the girls, making sure to get their faces, the lines of their bathing suits, which were so easy to miss. Tino, meanwhile, discovered the diving board. He didn't seem to know how to dive. But he jumped off it, slamming down on the end harder each time in order to get more height. "Enough jumping, Tino!" I called weakly. He ignored me—didn't even turn his head. *"No màs! No màs...saltar!"* I cried. It was pidgin Spanish, but I could tell he understood me because of the look in his eye: sheer impudence. "Tino! Stop!" My fear abated, and I grew irritated. If it had been my girls, I would have put a stop to it, shut it right down. He was yelling and splashing—it seemed obnoxious. So far, we four were alone at the pool. An older couple had walked past us on their way to the beach, leaving a wide, censorious berth—no one else. But I didn't want to make a scene. And if I really wanted to stop him, I would have to physically drag him away from the pool. Then people would surely take note. I sat immobile, watching as he ran and jumped and splashed. I kept looking around, scanning the terrace for other guests. There was only a uni-formed employee setting up glasses on the bar. It seemed safer to wait it out, pack up quietly come lunchtime. "He probably never gets to swim in a pool like this," I told my girls, who were practicing their underwater handstands and wanted me to rate them. "That's...an eight point five," I said distractedly. "Your legs were tilted. I'm glad he came with us," I lied. "It's the least we can do."

*   *   *

The next day, though, I resolved to say no if Reyna appeared with him again. It was too nerve-racking. I had lain awake thinking of how I would handle it if she asked, practicing the Spanish I would need to say no, though I thought it highly unlikely the boy would reappear. Surely she had sensed that the request was really a bit much. Surely she would not try to take advantage of my sympathy a second time. Confident in my predictions, I wasn't prepared for what happened. Tino arrived in a proper bathing suit, a blue Speedo—the day before he had worn his shorts—with a towel around his neck. He carried a large inflatable alligator. I pretended to have to go to the bathroom. When I emerged, I started to explain nervously to Reyna that today, it wasn't possible; today, I had plans to...I glanced over at Tino to see how he was taking it. He didn't protest— of course he didn't protest. He didn't so much as look at me. It was as if we hadn't spent the whole of yesterday morning together, as if he didn't even know who I was. It was that dullness in his expression that got me—the automatic acceptance, from so many years of practice, of the person in power saying no. An American kid would wail and whine, protest, throw a fit. I wanted to shake him and tell him to get mad at me, to shout that I was mean and awful and a terrible mother who didn't love him, as Celia often did. "*All* right," I said, dragging out the words with a good-natured show of reluctance. "One last day, okay? One more time! I leave Sunday! Tomorrow! But you have to be good, Tino, okay? You have to *listen* to me! *Tienes que escucharme!*"

*   *   *

It was asinine to try to elicit a promise from a seven-year-old. Still, I felt the sting of betrayal when we got down to the pool and he behaved in exactly the same manner as he had the day before—racing along the side of the pool to the deep end and jumping in before I said he could. *Boys,* I thought, blowing up Genie's arm floaties. *I don't know how to handle boys.* Today Genie and Celia just stood in the shallow end, watching the show. Tino improvised a routine in which he walked along the side of the pool nonchalantly, then suddenly pretended to fall into the water. My girls clapped in delight. He devised more elaborate iterations. He fell in sideways, backward. He had the natural showman's instinct to build on the performance to keep the audience engaged. The original conceit morphed into his walking the diving board and pretending he didn't realize when the board ended, at which point he would bat his hands and scissor his legs like a cartoon character walking off a cliff. When he got out and lay on his towel for five minutes, giggling, I realized I'd been gripped with fear since the moment we arrived at the pool. Now that I could relax for a second, I was angry as hell. I looked at my watch. *Five more minutes,* I said to myself. *Five more minutes.* I would make up an excuse—say I had a headache. Take them all back inside. I would sacrifice my girls' morning to put an end to this. *Dear God, just get me out of this. Get me the fuck out of this.* As if he knew his time was limited, Tino jumped up and darted back down to the diving board. He paused at the end, turned around, and—as my *No!* stuck in my throat—made a half-hearted attempt at a backflip but splashed down on his side.

"He's crazy," Celia said approvingly.

And then, just when I'd decided to put my foot down even if

it created a huge screaming temper tantrum—just when I was practicing in my head saying to Reyna, in no uncertain terms, *I* cannot *have him with me at the pool, do you understand? Do* not *bring him again,* the silvery-blond woman was back—she and the two men were having coffee at the bar. I had been so preoccupied watching Tino that I hadn't noticed them. Now that I had, I could feel the censure from twenty yards away.

"You have to be careful!" I said loudly in Spanish. I sounded pathetic, even to myself. But damned if I was going to give her the satisfaction of packing up in a hurry. Damned if I was going to sacrifice my principles to appease some petty snob whom I'd never see again. I sat back in my chair, folded my arms, and waited. Let her come and confront me—I'd give her a piece of my mind. *Go fuck yourself and your fancy condo.* I'd have it out with her, gladly. Then I'd deal with Tino—on my own terms. I glanced toward the bar. The opaque blue reflective sunglasses had turned to me. Now she was getting down from the stool. She was walking toward me, her face grimly set. I scrunched up bits of my towel in my hands. She was going to yell at me— I was about to become the object of public scorn and censure. *Let her. Just let her!* Whatever she said, it didn't matter—I would soon be home. I would apologize to Vero, and I would never see these people again. It would also work to my advantage, I realized; I'd be able to tell Reyna that it wasn't my fault I could no longer bring her grandson to the pool, that I had gotten yelled at—RESIDENTS ONLY was for real. Tino paused, grinning, at the end of the diving board. The board thwanged as he jumped up in the air and came down. *One,* I thought, gritting my teeth. *"Oye!"* cried the woman. She raised a hand and pointed at the boy—she broke into a run. Tino jumped up and came down. *Two.* "*Oye, chico!*" He jumped up and went so high, it was as if he didn't know what to do with the extra time in the air, the profligacy of space. He was up there ecstatically twisting his body for seconds, it seemed, basking in the joy of his athleticism. I was already hearing the splash in my head when instead, there was a terrible cracking sound. A crack as his head hit the corner of the board. A shockingly loud crack before he bounced off the board into the water. I knew as fast as I knew when Celia broke her arm jumping off a swing set in Central Park. I was out of my chair and into the deep end. It took me the count of one second, maybe two. Two strokes and my arms were around his body, encircling the slim, slippery torso. I was dragging him, humping his body over the side of the pool, a nonstop scream coming out of my mouth: "Help! Help! Help! Help! Help!" I pushed his legs up out of the water. The silvery-blond woman was already there, kneeling down, to receive him. I heard shouting behind her in Spanish, but she was calm—utterly focused. She was crouching, breathing into his mouth. I flung myself out of the pool. "I was—I was—"

"No!" With one cutting gesture, she banished me from her side. It was like the gesture you use to shame a dog who's gotten into the dinner.

One of the men from the bar had rushed over too. "Don't worry," he said kindly to me in English. "She's a doctor."

I stared at him. *Worry?* I thought. *Worry?*

I sat on my chair at the end of the pool with my arms around the girls. Tino sputtered and coughed, but he was still unconscious. There was shouting back and forth to the bar. "Can't I call an ambulance?" I kept pleading. No one took me up on the offer, but a few minutes later, an ambulance arrived. As the EMTs were loading Tino into it, Reyna appeared on the run, bellowing and clutching at her apron. The blond woman knew her—she called her by her name in the harshest tone. She upbraided her; she sounded outraged. Reyna hid her face in her apron and moaned. The doctor would ride in the ambulance with Tino. She was hopping into the back, issuing orders as the doors closed. One of the men ran over and handed up her purse. The other man beckoned—he would take Reyna in his car. She trundled after him. I had nothing to do with any of it. I wanted to get the address of the hospital but it would have slowed them down if I'd asked.

I gave the girls Saltines for dinner, and tuna out of a can. We stared at the television. I tried to call a couple of hospitals but I couldn't figure out how to dial the numbers. I knew how to call the United States but I kept getting an error and a dial tone when I tried anything local. I finally got through to a person but when I tried to explain, the line went dead. I didn't even know Tino's last name—I didn't know Reyna's. There could have been a dozen hospitals in Acapulco. There was no way to explain. I opened the condo door and looked out on the walkway but I was too afraid to go and knock next door—what good would it do anyway? I put the girls to bed, telling them in a serious but cheerful voice that Tino was getting the best possible care. I slept maybe forty-five minutes, waking just before dawn. I succumbed to one of those crazy-mom impulses—I woke up Genie and Celia and made them get dressed so we could walk on the beach as the sun rose. We'd been saying we would all week, and this was our last chance—our last day. It was now or never. They went complaining, but once we were out there, they saw how special it was to be up so early on the deserted beach.

As soon as we got back to the condo, I started to pack, throwing clothes and shoes and paperbacks into my suitcase in a frenzy even though the car to the airport wouldn't come till noon. When I was nearly ready and was looking around the living room for the items I had forgotten, I remembered the passports. The passports the security guard had taken. "The passports!" I said. "They never returned the passports!" Celia and Genie looked up from the floor, where they were playing with their stuffed animals. "Oh, yeah," Celia said, "I forgot to tell you—they said that they can't give them back yet."

"What?" I began to interrogate her. "When? Who? Who said that? Where was I?" My daughter shrugged and, clearly bored by the questions, turned back to the game. That's when I heard the door rattle. "Oh my God, it's the police!" I blurted out. The girls looked at me. I pressed the back of my hand to my mouth. Perhaps I truly was cracking up. I stared at the door, praying for I don't know what. I heard the key turning in the lock. *Reyna*, I thought. *Oh my God, it's Reyna.* I was aghast. She was coming to work—coming to work as usual. What on earth would I say to her? What words would I use? I dug my nails into my palms. I would not shirk my responsibility. I would not try to gloss over the incident. Whatever had happened—I would deal with it.

"*Buenos días,* Reyna," I cried as the door was pushed open.

A petite woman with her hair up in a bun and a quick, cross

manner came in. She didn't look at me as she went to stow her bag in the cleaning closet.

"Perdóname, perdóname!"

Trying to get my bearings, I followed her from the closet into the kitchen, where she pulled on a pair of rubber yellow gloves. "Tino, Tino—the little boy! *El nieto de* Reyna?" I said. *"Cómo está? Cómo está el niño?"* She stood with her back to the sink, not listening, it was clear, just waiting. *"Se fue en una ambulancia?"* I tried with increasing agitation. "Yesterday?"

I asked her ten different ways. I mentioned the pool, the accident. "Reyna!" I said. "Where is Reyna now?" I pantomimed swimming, a blow to the head. I made the sound of the ambulance siren. She watched me expressionlessly. It was as if my voice had been muted for all the effect on her it had. Long before I finished, the woman turned her back to me and turned on the water. She began to do the breakfast dishes.

Failing at English, I cried in frustration, "Do you even speak *Spanish?*" When she didn't answer, I went up right next to her and said, "Excuse me! Ex*cuse* me! Who sent you here today? Can you just answer me that, please? What are you *doing* here?" When she still ignored me, I cried, "Who even *are* you? Hello-o! Is anyone home? Do you have a name? Do you have a fucking name?" I grabbed her by the shoulder, and I shook it. "Who are you? Where is Reyna? Reyna knows me! She knows me! Can you just fucking tell me what's going on? Why are you here?"

The Little Rats

At the last minute, the money was found for Hannah to go on the French trip. It was late to sign on. From where she sat at the kitchen table, tearing vengefully at her cuticles as she listened to her father's side of the conversation, Hannah gathered that Madame Giraud had protested but did not say no. By now, the Beales had missed the meeting at school at which the trip had been discussed in detail, the schedule gone over, the emergency numbers given out. In the two weeks leading up to the girls' departure for Paris, Hannah kept finding out what seemed to be critical information by chance—when Catherine Beier mentioned how cold Madame Giraud had reminded them Paris was in March, for instance. "It's latitude forty-eight— the same as Newfoundland," Catherine said when she and Hannah were the last ones finishing lunch one day. The other girls had already hurried out to the back garden despite how cold Massachusetts, north of Boston, was in March.

This was "historic" Massachusetts. It wasn't unusual for a Country Day girl's family to have a connection to the colonists' revolt, which had started down the road. By eighth grade, the last year in the school, most of the girls had seen so many reenactments of Paul Revere's ride, they had a preference for the bay horse that was used some years over the chestnut. Hannah was from Musketaquid—farther out. Musketaquid was also a Revolutionary War town but not one anyone made much of. Most of the girls in Hannah's class were Kates, meaning they had been at the school from K through eight, though some said the term derived from the name of the founder of Pembridge Country Day, Katharine Wilcox Berry. Hannah was not a Kate—not even close. She had been at PCD only a year and a half, which sometimes struck her as rather pathetic.

"Did Madame say anything else?" Hannah asked worriedly as they crumpled their crusts and tinfoil into their paper bags. She got the bucket and sponge and wiped the table while Catherine swept under the chairs. At Country Day, the girls also washed the blackboards, rinsed the snack plates and cups, and tidied the classrooms. There was much more work than at Hannah's old, public school, though that was an irony, like so many, that didn't strike her till much later. Anyway, you could argue that in her case, the irony didn't really apply: she was attending the private girls' school on 70 percent financial aid.

Catherine Beier was a serious girl—the smartest in their class, with a German émigré professor for a father and a single unvarying braid down her back. She could be trusted to give serious answers, not like the more popular girls—

Wendy, Jessica, Emmy Duke—who turned any question about the trip into speculation on which one of them would get to make out with Fred Standish on the *bateau-mouche*. (Wendy Waxman, it was generally acknowledged.) Per a decade-long tradition, the trip was being taken with the boys from their brother school, Lincoln. Besides Fred, hands down the best-looking, and his friend and sidekick, Marty Biddle, Hannah had only fleeting impressions, from the few dances there'd been, of the boys who were going on the trip. She wasn't in carpools with them. She didn't go to dancing school at the Pembridge town hall. She didn't have an older brother who'd gone to Lincoln. At the dances, she had danced in a group with other girls during the fast songs and ridden home alone to Musketaquid with her father, who at least did not expect her to talk.

"Only that Madame Giraud and Madame Dumas are matching us up together with the teachers from Paris," Catherine said as they headed out to the garden to join the others. Madame Giraud was their teacher, Madame Dumas the Lincoln boys'—known to the girls as a stricter, more exacting substitute. Hannah, who was quick at impressions, did a funny one of the latter. L'amour *ce n'est pas* la mort, *les filles! Ce ne sont pas les mêmes choses!*

"The teachers are comparing notes," Catherine explained, "so we each end up with the best Parisian *correspondante* for us."

"I wonder how they'll match me," fretted Hannah. "I joined so late." The two of them stood leaning against the garden wall watching Hilary Thompkins and the other athletic girls play four square. "I'll probably get some awful French girl. Some bottom-of-the-barrel girl no one else wanted."

*　　*　　*

"We eat!" Dominique Lefebvre announced a week later, pointing a finger at her open mouth. Through the fog of the jet lag, Hannah smiled and nodded, trying to be cooperative. *"Très bien!"*

It was funny how you could tell, even in another language, that she and Dominique would never have been friends. Her *correspondante* was impatient; preoccupied; shrill. No intellectual, she. The only books in the Lefebvres' apartment as far as Hannah could tell were a set of encyclopedias displayed on the shelf above the television. Sitting on an overstuffed, rust-colored sofa, she struggled to make conversation with the girl as Madame Lefebvre cooked lunch in a tiny back kitchen. Hannah's difficulty was not with the French but with finding a topic that would last more than a sentence or two. Dominique did not seem to want to meet her halfway and cut all her inquiries short.

"What arrondissement are we in?" Hannah asked in French, though she already knew.

"Ze twelve."

The air in the small apartment was stuffy with stale cigarette smoke. Hannah's eyelids were so heavy that she was afraid she might actually nod off.

"What is your favorite subject in school?"

"Mathematics."

Still…she had made it to Paris! No matter that Dominique's apartment building—modern and charmless, with a garage underneath and a dilapidated elevator—was not at all how she had pictured it. Already the dark truncated night on the plane was forgotten, the corralling at Logan Airport beforehand, where the Lincoln boys and Country Day girls had stood in two groups, titillatingly close, having shed their parents as fast as they could.

"We'll miss you so much, honey," Jan had choked out, pressing crumpled-up tissues to her eyes. Hannah's father was outside circling in the car so as not to pay for parking. Hannah couldn't quite bring herself to desert her mother before the flight was called, knowing it would have crushed her, but she also could not find it in herself to be gracious to Jan, despite the fact that it was her double shifts at the hospital that would pay for the trip. As Hannah waited beside her, Mrs. Turner, the head of the PTA, appeared with Libby and her twin brother, Bruce. She scanned the crowd and accosted Emmy Duke's mother. "For once, I'm going to have time for the dogs and the horses—now that these two rug rats are out of my hair!"

It was March break that the girls were "sacrificing" to go to Paris. Hilary Thompkins, who ski-raced every weekend in New Hampshire, had almost not been allowed to go. "My dad's not speaking to me!" she boomed happily, standing in the middle of the gaggle of girls, towering over them, just as she did playing center when they had basketball in gym—or "sports," as Country Day styled it. Wendy Waxman's mother turned to Madame Giraud and murmured, "Don't tell a soul, but Phil and I are sneaking away to St. Thomas for a week. Anything for a bit of sun!"

*   *   *

In the small bedroom the girls would share for the duration of the visit, Dominique would sleep on a foldout cot, ceding her bed to Hannah. Discovering this and now looking around the cramped living room—taking in its vases of fake flowers, the two fancy armchairs covered in plastic—Hannah could admit to a sense of relief. She no longer had to worry that she would have to apologize for her own house. When Dominique came to the States in April for the second half of the exchange, the French girl would have the guest room to herself.

"We eat!" Dominique repeated, pointing at her mouth.

"Oui, oui," Hannah said curtly. The repetition—particularly in English—incensed her. Perhaps Dominique thought she was an idiot who couldn't understand a word of French. With her pinched little face and the long, greasy-looking dark hair that hung down her back, Dominique was not what Hannah had pictured either. She sat on the sofa just so, her posture exaggeratedly correct, like a marionette whose strings have been pulled just until taut, and her face moved in a prescribed, didactic fashion as, without a hint of embarrassment, she began to lecture Hannah on the cultural attractions of Paris. "You will go to ze Louvre, where one can find…" Beside her, Hannah felt like a whale beached on the sofa cushions. She felt enormous—slow and blond and pink, pointlessly clean and scrubbed.

Perhaps the feeling of surprise was mutual. In the arrivals section at Roissy, Dominique and her mother had looked at Hannah in confusion when she stepped forward from the group of kids, dragging her suitcase, that American eagerness to like and be liked no doubt written all over her face. A terse exchange had ensued between mother and daughter—an accusation made; an insistence, Hannah inferred, on Madame Lefebvre's part, that it wasn't her fault. Doing her best to ignore this, Hannah had watched giggling, never-serious Wendy Waxman snapping photos with her large, impeccably dressed host family, the glamorous mother in pumps and a long coat and scarf, the father debonair in a suit and tie although it was Saturday. The daughter Clotilde, Wendy's *correspondante*, had already aroused much interest on the part of the Lincoln boys. The jokester Marty Biddle was attempting to introduce himself to her—and getting mocked by Wendy for doing so— when, with an abrupt *"Hopla!"* Dominique seized Hannah's hard case. Despite the impediment—she insisted on carrying it—she threaded her way rapidly through the airport to the car park. It was like following a small animal going to ground. Hannah race-walked and trotted to keep up, feeling cross and a bit confused. When they had to pause for an elevator, the tiny Madame Lefebvre—she could not have been more than four eleven—smiled but did not look at her, as if she felt guilty about something.

Now pausing in her lecture (topic: the region of Montmartre), Dominique took a long bobby pin from her pocket and stuck it in her mouth. With quick expert fingers, she wrapped her hair into a coil and pinned it up. Impressed, Hannah caught her eye. Her own hands must have been the most unskilled in all of Country Day. She couldn't even French-braid; she rotated three headbands to keep her thick hair off her face. Supervising the decoration for the winter-themed dance at school, Libby's mother, Mrs. Turner, had poked fun at the snowflakes she'd cut out—"Well, that's a forlorn little flake if I ever saw one, Hannah!" Libby Turner was the best artist in the class, but all of Country Day seemed to excel at crafts—girls could embroider and crochet and paint watercolors.

"*Tu danses?*" Hannah guessed. Watching Dominique do her hair, she had suddenly put it together—the exaggeratedly correct posture, the way she'd stood at the airport, her feet turned out, rising up and down on her toes.

For the first time that day, Dominique seemed to drop the mask of condescension. She glanced quickly at Hannah—she looked uncomfortable. "Yes, I do…big dance." Hannah's *correspondante* seemed to search for other words but then said again, more doubtfully, "I do…very big dance!" She sounded so unsure of herself, one might have assumed she was lying, but Hannah sensed what it really was. The seriousness of her commitment made it impossible for her to speak of it to a layperson—she couldn't have even if she'd had the English words. Hannah, who understood precisely this kind of single-minded sacrifice, let the subject drop.

"We eat!" Dominique announced again, clapping her hands together, the artifice back. For the third or fourth time, she opened her mouth and pointed at it. "We eat!"

"*J'ai compris! On va manger!*" Hannah said shortly in her best accent. She felt a prick of dismay when she thought of spending two weeks with this pedantic little person.

"We eat!" Dominique said again, undeterred.

"*J'ai compris!*" Hannah fairly shouted. The French girl shook her head in a noiseless laugh. She looked like a little rat when she laughed, her features scrunched up and twitching.

When Dominique rose to help her mother in the kitchen, Hannah stared at the overflowing ashtray on the coffee table, repulsed yet fascinated. She could imagine Libby or Wendy saying brightly, *Excuse me, could you please open a window? The smoke bothers me!*, feeling well within her rights. For Hannah, it was different. It was as if she had signed a contract coming here; now she must try to be French.

Bearded and heavyset, with a shapeless dark sweater pulled down over a sizable paunch, Monsieur Lefebvre kissed Hannah on each cheek. As Dominique chastised him and brushed crumbs off his sweater, he held Hannah's gaze and said, with great effort, "Welcome. To. Paris." His eyes were bright blue and twinkled, making Hannah ashamed that she had recoiled from his pungent body odor, his sharp breath.

"On mange!" Madame Lefebvre said simply, removing her apron and wearing the same embarrassed smile as she emerged from the kitchen to call them to the table. Covered in plastic when Hannah arrived, it was now laid with a heavy brocade tablecloth, a wineglass at each place—including, Hannah noted, her own.

"For dinner, we eat!" Dominique said, pointing at a plate of meat.

"Très bien!" Hannah fairly snapped. *"Je suis très faim!"*

Dominique's correction was instantaneous. *"J'ai très faim,"* she said in just the pedantic tone Madame Giraud would have used. *"Pas 'je suis,' 'Annah."*

It didn't seem fair! The little rat had been making huge, glaring mistakes in English every time she opened her mouth—calling lunch "dinner" a second ago, for example.

With Dominique's rebuke, Hannah felt the adrenaline she had been going on ebb all at once. An unexpected pang of homesickness struck her. Eyes smarting, she cut up her meat and took a bite. The texture was unusual—not at all what she'd expected. It was…rubbery, as if she'd bitten into a piece that was entirely cartilage. She managed to keep chewing for a moment, but then she gagged and had to hide it with her fist to her mouth—pretending to cough, then choking it down. Despite the elaborate table setting, there were no napkins. Her eyes flew up to Dominique's. "Tongue!" she exclaimed, breaking into English. "That's what you meant: 'We eat *tongue!*'"

Dominique's eyes and nose crinkled as she went into her silent laugh. The exaggerated little clapping motion she made—that, too, was just like a gesture Madame Giraud would have made, the fingers of one hand tapping neatly against the base of the other palm. *"Oui!"* Something-something *"enfin,"* she said— you finally got it. *"On mange de la langue."* She explained the misunderstanding to her father, gesticulating as she drew out the story. Monsieur Lefebvre listened, nodding soberly, then burst into laughter. Hannah could see bits of food in his mouth as he threw his head back. Monsieur and Madame Lefebvre laughed till they wiped their eyes, starting up over and over. At home, Hannah took after Jan—she could be sensitive to slights, over-ashamed of mistakes. Scenes often ended with Hannah's crying, "And now I'll never live it down!"—Jan wringing her hands outside a slammed door. But now, in this foreign country, so far from home, another possibility seemed to present itself; it was as if it had wafted in with the puff of cold air from the window that Dominique, noting Hannah rubbing at her eyes as she took her seat, had jacked open, again chastising her parents, this time for smoking: *"Une habitude dégoûtante!"* *All right, then!* Hannah thought, no longer offended but game for any and all of it. She grinned and showed her teeth—

a smile, the Lefebvres remarked, speaking to one another, not to her, that was *"Très très américain—américain classique, n'est-ce pas?"*

Thirty years later, Hannah sits in an Upper West Side café nursing an unwanted coffee on a cold spring afternoon as the shiny-bright young woman across from her gives her her pitch. Dana is her name. She brims with the early-to-bed energy of the entry-level professional—seems proud to introduce herself as the "junior development officer" at Pembridge Country Day. Dana Purnick, soon to be Purnick-Murray. "We've decided to hyphenate," she says demurely, twisting a modest solitaire diamond on her finger. Dana herself is not a Country Day alum—they established this early. "Nope!" She giggles. "I was public school all the way!" The laugh seems to hold a touch of shame, but perhaps a touch of pride as well. She appears, to Hannah, ridiculously young. There's an innocence to her unfashionable white blouse, which Hannah associates with Boston, to her straight skirt and pumps, her repeated references to her "fiancé," a word Hannah would have assumed had gone out of fashion long ago. In a reverential tone, she explains to Hannah that the current Country Day parent body is "kind of crazy." When Hannah is mystified, not understanding what she's getting at, Dana clarifies, apologetically, "Now that the venture-cap money has come to town."

"Ah," Hannah says. "Ah."

* * *

Hannah isn't sure why she agreed to this meeting when Dana Purnick from development reached out over e-mail. No one else would have, she suspects—not even the handful of her classmates who do give to the school. In their forties, they are too busy with jobs, children, and—if they're honest—their husbands' jobs; with holding the fort. Hannah has a job and a grade-school-age son, a proposal for an academic book due, a modest country house with a major termite problem, a husband who's suddenly in demand at cardiothoracic conferences, and an old, failing dog at home, but she, apparently, is not too busy to say yes to junior development officer Dana Purnick's offer to "walk you through some of the changes at PCD." Her mind flits over the guilt, gratitude, obligations, and, ultimately, the self-congratulatory impulse that brought her here as the young woman launches into her spiel. *See how far I've come?*

Hannah's alma mater, Dana excitedly informs her, has installed a green roof over the new regulation-size gymnasium. She names a noted architect responsible for its design—"I'm sure you know, he's actually the grandfather of a current student, a sixth-grader."

Hannah had not known but says obligingly, "Oh, wow. That's great." It's funny how they think you'll be interested in all of this. She stirs her coffee to distract herself from the exasperating tediousness of the conversation as Dana goes giddily on—"state-of-the-art," "impactful," "pedagogical research has shown," all intoned like numbers in a game of development-office bingo.

Of course, Hannah thinks, Country Day has joined the facilities race, has succumbed to the fancier-the-better fallacy—the same fallacy that drove a fundraising campaign at her son's private school this past winter. If Hannah were to go back today, she probably wouldn't recognize the place. The original building, a clapboard colonial house plus an annex where she and her classmates spent the entire school day, might look a bit like those wooden houses that remain on one or two streets in Manhattan among the high-rises. But Hannah isn't one of those alums who keep in close touch with the school, this meeting notwithstanding. She has never gone back, and now that Jan and her father have moved to a retirement community in North Carolina to escape the Massachusetts winters, she probably never will. It's not as if she's making a statement by not returning. Returning to a place you'd spent but two years— that, Hannah thinks, would be the statement.

Dutifully, she studies the photos in the binder Dana flips through with her perfectly manicured hands: the black-box theater, the "professional-quality" darkroom, the indoor/outdoor greenhouse. The ceramics studio, she is somehow gratified to see, was given by Libby Turner and her wife, who, she recalls from her Christmas-card list, live in Pembridge.

"It's funny," Hannah ventures, "when you think that we used to have lunch in the gym. And it was the theater too." Dana goes to reply, but not to be deterred, Hannah adds firmly, "And the assembly room! Anything and everything took place in that one big room."

For a moment, the voluble Dana has nothing to say. She closes the binder and leans down to stow it in her soft brief-case. Sitting back up, she looks past Hannah when she says, "Some alums have been more interested in the reimagination of the *old* gym as a fully integrated maker space where joint projects—"

"Oh God!" Hannah interrupts. "I loathed group projects!" She speaks with good humor, not badgering or angry, but Dana blinks rapidly, the way you do when someone who has power over you says something hurtful. "I hated worrying about whether the other kids would drag my grade down! In our day," Hannah adds gleefully, "the class was ranked."

"I—"

"Catherine Beier was number one."

"Catherine...sorry. Catherine? I don't think I—" Dana stops, flustered. Perhaps her job training hasn't prepared her to deal with the recalcitrant alum. She takes a moment to compose herself. When she continues, she speaks in a different tone. She is assertive now, even snippy. "I don't know if you've had time to read Dr. Barnwell's updated mission statement, but it is the mandate of Country Day to encourage *collaboration* over *competition*. A key, ahem, success factor—"

"I was number two."

"—in today's knowledge economy. Oh, yeah? Were you?" Dana smiles uncertainly. "Well, that's great!"

A more seasoned "officer" would probably pick up on the hint this is—go off-script and ask about Hannah's experience. Say, *Tell me more about Country Day when you were there*—those simple words that magically open pocketbooks. It occurs to Hannah for the second time that the impulse to take this meeting was far from altruistic. Take the meeting, implying you'll give the money...and let the sucking-up begin. That was the idea, wasn't it? Hannah's department, comp. lit., has been riven by the most petty politics this year. Maybe she just wanted to relive her eighth-grade glory days, have someone remind her of all her achievements, from back when achievement was clean—the full ride to St. Paul's, Harvard, the PhD, which she would then, of course, deprecate, with false modesty.

Dana Purnick, however, has moved on to languages—or not languages themselves but the new language *labs*. Hannah perks up, nodding and doing her best not to interrupt. It's only when Dana finally runs out of "features" to name that Hannah jumps in. "Do you still have the French trip?"

Funny that she doesn't know—she has never read the alumnae magazine carefully enough to check. There had been a moment, several years ago, when it looked as if she might be moving back. Arvind's mentor at Harvard was trying to get him to come to Mass. General; she'd been keeping tabs on a tenure-track position at B.U. She had thought she might be back in all of that. Her son, Dev, would go to Lincoln, and she'd go around saying, "Now, when *I* was at Country Day..."— being supremely annoying, really. She was already fantasizing about the Mercedes wagon with the matching wheel caps like the one Mrs. Turner had driven when, in order to keep her husband at Columbia, the administration had offered him chief of the division. That seemed fair enough; Arvind was more ambitious than she was. Of late, Hannah had realized she lacked real vision—her husband had it in spades, whereas she had only ever wanted to get so far.

Meant as a softball, the French-trip inquiry doesn't seem to be a simple question with an easy answer. Poor Dana looks tense. "The what?" she says tightly.

"The trip to Paris. With Lincoln?"

"I'm not sure, actually. I'm actually not sure." Dana shuffles the development materials in front of her on the café table, looking as if at any minute she might take her bat and ball and go home.

"Really?" Hannah is honestly taken aback. "Gosh, I thought that trip would never die. It was such a hallmark of our Country Day experience."

"Oh, wait! Wait!" The young woman has forgotten herself and is now pointing aggressively at Hannah's sternum. "I do know what you mean! The French students—yes! They do a weekend in Montreal! That must be it. They *do* do a trip."

"Oh…" Hannah absorbs this. "So it's Montreal now?"

"I'm pretty sure no one goes to France," Dana says flatly. Hannah reads her irritation and doesn't, she finds, blame her for it. Entitled alum bent on reliving her glory days. What a grind it must all be, alleviated only by the fun of the venture-cap money having come to town.

"Is it with Lincoln?"

"I'm sorry?"

"The Montreal trip," she says as gently as she can. "Do they go with the boys?"

"Um—*no*. No, they don't. I do remember this, actually. So, I came in 2015? I started in admissions? You wouldn't have seen me on the development roster till 2017."

"I see." Hannah is touched by the idea that Dana thinks she would have noticed.

"Yeah, I didn't make the move to development till 2017. Anyway, I remember the decision was made that the boys were undermining the trip. There was a lot of, you know…horsing around, I think it was." She turns her palms up—surrendering. "I mean, I don't know! Don't quote me or anything. Nothing *happened*."

"Okay..."

"Phew, right? But the point was, it's a great leadership opportunity for the girls. Two days looking around Montreal—yes, that's awesome. But the highlight? It's really the last day. Everyone says it's the highlight. It's almost like—" Dana casts her eyes up in a moment of shy hesitation. "It's almost like a corporate off-site?" she says reverently. "They have breakout groups? And they work on leadership skills? It's so incredible what they do on that trip. I can't believe I blanked on it! Jeez, Louise! It's an amazing trip!"

Several responses suggest themselves to Hannah. After a moment, she only says mildly, "It sounds it."

"What do you think?" Catherine asked Hannah as they mounted the steps of La Madeleine behind the Lincoln boys. The outings for the Americans had started right away, the Monday after they arrived. Hannah followed her gaze to Fred Standish, fetching in a red Shetland sweater that made him look as if his mother still dressed him—she probably did, she and Catherine had concurred. "Was he sprung fully gorgeous from the smoke machine at the Lincoln gym?"

Hannah gave a laugh because Catherine's joke was clever, but at the top of the stairs she fiddled with her camera, advancing the film to the next picture. She often felt, waspishly, that because Catherine did not really participate, she fell to narrating everything.

The girls were giddy as they waited in the queue to enter the temple-like church. The sweeping views of Paris, the grand Corinthian columns, and the boys, the boys whom they were starting to know—Fred, Marty, Bruce Turner, Byron Suh, the two Davids—by name and, like the saints in the paintings, by the objects they carried that seemed to symbolize them: Fred with the sweaters, Marty with the backward baseball cap, Byron scribbling in a little book...

"The maid caught me in bed this morning!" thundered Hilary Thompkins.

"They brought me hot chocolate when I woke up!"

"Clotilde and I have the top floor all to ourselves!"

"Monsieur Bernier works at the Musée d'Orsay! *Il est*...curator! We got a private tour!"

"Françoise's parents own a bookstore," Catherine told Hannah as they waited. "Isn't that funny? Must have been the closest Madame Giraud could find to academics. They keep giving me books to take home for *mon père le professeur*. I'll never be able to fit them all! But how's yours? *Ça va bien?*"

"*Oui! C'est un appartement. Cinquième étage...*" Hannah's voice trailed off. That was all she could think of to say. At least Catherine would know that *she* knew that the Parisian fifth floor was *their* sixth floor. They were careful about things like that—detail-oriented, the both of them. The two girls were academic rivals, but Catherine had the edge. She was good at every subject, studious and matter-of-fact. There was no drama to her As in algebra, no Jan doing dishes and fretting, "I wish I could help!," while Hannah wept and her father accused her of not focusing—of not trying to understand.

There was a lull in the shouting and carrying-on as the group advanced toward the entrance to the church. Hannah blurted out, perhaps intending to be overheard, "Dominique's a dancer!"

"And what did you and Dominique do this weekend, Hannah?" Madame Giraud asked her in French.

She didn't want to talk about what they had done Saturday and then again, Sunday afternoon, after Dominique got home from ballet, so she went on, "My *correspondante* is a big ballet dancer. She's going to be a professional." This last point, which was her own, she made rather defensively, mentally daring any of them to challenge her on it.

"Does she go to the Paris Opera Ballet school?" This was placid, smiley Emmy Duke. With her brown eyes, her braids, and the permanent flush on her cheeks, she was Holly Hobbie to Hannah. She also had the largest breasts in the class. All anatomies were known to the girls due to their changing for sports in one big room.

Hannah hesitated. "Um—yes, she does, actually," she said. "That's where she goes."

"My mom's been to the Paris Opera Ballet!" Emmy said. "She says it's amazing." This was something Hannah already knew—Emmy had made the same remark when they learned about the famous ballet because their textbook featured it in one of its cultural asides, *Allons au Ballet!*

"I love ballet," Emmy breathed, talking close to Hannah as she always did. "I'd love to be a dancer."

"Could we go?" asked Libby Turner. "That would be such fun. Madame Giraud? Madame Giraud? Can we go to the ballet while we're here?"

"You guys are into ballet?" said Marty Biddle, poker-faced under the baseball hat. If handsome Fred Standish had been cast in the role of husband at umpteen sleepovers, short but dogged Marty was who you ended up with as a joke. "And then

189

you married Marty Biddle and had five children" always got a snort and a laugh.

"Yes! We are, Marty!" Libby sneered back. "Do you have a problem with the fact that some of us enjoy the arts?"

"My package in tights!" was overheard as they filed through the entrance at last.

Cupping their crotches and plié-ing, the boys peeled off into hysteria. Madame Dumas backhanded Marty and spit out, *"Taisez-vous, enfin! Pensez à l'image des américains que vous donnez!,"* but rather than the teacher's threat, the magnificent domed interior of the church was what silenced the lot of them.

What Hannah had done on Saturday afternoon hadn't involved a museum—couldn't really be called a cultural outing. After lunch, Dominique had told her they would go out. Outside on rue du Moulin, the day had grown grayer and the wind was up. Hannah stuffed her hands into the shallow pockets of her short wool coat. She had ignored Madame Giraud's advice, favoring fashion over practicality, and left her old parka at home in Musketaquid. Seeing Catherine in hers at the airport, she'd wanted to yank it off her—to cry, *At least pretend that this is the chance of a lifetime! At least pretend that this trip could change everything!*

They walked along Dominique's street to an elevated highway, where they waited by the entrance to a pedestrian underpass. Despite the cold, Hannah looked around happily, like a dumb American who was willing to be pleased by anything— by the white-on-blue street signs affixed to the buildings, by the window of the boulangerie-patisserie, filled with napoleons and tarts, by the severe grandmother in a black coat and hat who shot them a disapproving look as she passed. She was in Paris—she was in Paris, and it was as if the idea of Paris had been inside of her always. *Oh, yes, of course,* she kept thinking—when Dominique swept crumbs off the luncheon table with a little tool, when Madame Lefebvre poured a Coke for her out of a different kind of bottle with a different label than it had at home—*there* that *is.*

Dominique held her arms in front of her—one straight out, the other bent at the elbow—and switched them back and forth. She rose up on her toes. "My friend—'e come," she said to Hannah.

"Do you go to the Paris Opera Ballet?" Hannah asked. She wanted confirmation so she could revisit the subject with Emmy Duke. But Dominique's little face flinched as if she'd been struck.

"We learned about it in school!" Hannah said apologetically. *"Nous l'avons étudié."*

"Non, you see...I—go late. I..." Eyes downcast, Dominique spoke painfully slowly, insisting on making the complicated explanation in English. "My mother—she don't know...she don't know nothing, you see..." She looked pleadingly up at Hannah. "I am old." An adult, Hannah knew, would make a sarcastic joke out of Dominique's referring to herself as "old." But Hannah understood. Oh, she understood full well. As her *correspondante* went on in her halting English, she recalled the moment in seventh grade when, sitting at lunch in her new school, she found out about the Kates designation—Libby Turner's saying, "You see, we will all have been here from K through eight," the moment she internalized that it was something even the hardest work, even the greatest academic

success, would never afford her. It was too late for her to ever be a Kate.

"Yes, I am very old," Dominique said, regretful as an old woman, "but I try this summer." She smiled sadly at Hannah. "I try for *les petits rats*."

"*Les…*" Confused momentarily, Hannah cried out when she remembered. "Oh my God, of course! *Les petits rats! Les petits rats de l'Opéra*." It was the name for the full-time students—the ones who had been selected as the up-and-coming ballerinas. Madame Giraud had spent half a class having fun with the name. Perhaps Hannah had subconsciously been thinking of that all along.

"Ze little rats," Dominique translated.

Hannah raised her eyes to the gray sky. "Yup—got that." She pictured herself insisting on answering only in French—as retaliation for Dominique's pedantry—when the little rat came to the U.S. in April. She was chuckling to herself at the Monty Python absurdity of it when a young man in a leather jacket appeared, trotting up the stairs.

Lightly hurrying, hands buried in the jacket, he cocked his head back when he saw them but didn't break into a smile. His seriousness hit Hannah like a physical revelation.

He had dark brown hair that waved back from a chiseled face that Hannah would be reminded of later in the trip, when they went to Sacré-Coeur, where the caricature artists sat— the exaggerated angles of chin and nose and forehead. He might have been seventeen. Thierry was his name. He seemed to have as little to do with the Lincoln boys as the cooked lunch she had just eaten had to do with her mother's peanut butter and jelly on Pepperidge Farm white. She wished she could take a picture of him for Wendy, who was "obsessed, just obsessed, totally fucking obsessed" with James Dean. He kissed Dominique hello. Then it was Hannah's turn. He leaned over her as Monsieur Lefebvre had, holding his cheek steady—she was the one who had to turn her head from side to side. He, too, was a smoker, she realized, blushing.

"'E does James Dean," Dominique told Hannah matter-of-factly.

"He…"

"'E try to look like James Dean."

The frankness of the admission made Hannah look away. "Well, I'd say…*t'as réussi!*" she said to Thierry.

The posse of Lincoln boys would laugh and joke and swear and squeal; push one another, tap you on the shoulder and then hide, bump you, stop short in front of you, crowd you. They were never still; it was against their religion to be serious. Thierry was nothing like them. Thierry was self-possessed— Thierry watched Dominique carefully, not saying a word. Why, he's in love with her, Hannah realized. With a shrug, he seemed to demur about making a decision on a question Dominique had posed to him. She made an exasperated noise and led them back the way they had come. When they should have turned for her apartment on the rue du Moulin, they walked on past the street.

It fell to Hannah to keep up the conversation. She asked silly, touristic questions about the neighborhood, the arrondisse-ment, arrondissements in general, that Dominique answered at length and with no trace of humor. Occasionally Thierry would venture an opinion, and she would correct him. "No—not the eighteenth century, the seventeenth," Hannah translated. "*Non, ce n'était pas Philippe Le Bel. C'était Philippe Trois! Tu ne sais rien.*" He played the same role as Dominique's parents, she saw—he was benighted, as everyone in Dominique's world was, and needed Dominique to speak English for him, to liaise with the world at large. They rounded a corner; the entrance to a vast public park was suddenly before them. Hannah glimpsed water in the near distance, the landscape stretching out beyond it—paths, benches, rolling sections of lawn, a real wood.

"Le Bois de Vincennes," announced Dominique in her docent's voice. She indicated the park, making a balletic gesture with her hand.

For a long time, it seemed to Hannah, though it was probably no more than fifteen or twenty minutes, the three of them walked down a footpath with a pond to their right. Dominique and her boyfriend walked arm in arm, like a mature married couple, strolling along despite the rawness of the day. Surreptitiously, Hannah turned up the collar of her jacket, buried her hands deeper in her pockets. The French teenagers conversed laconically, the five-franc tour of Paris forgotten. Hannah felt like their child—they didn't pay too much attention to her, but if she strayed, she felt sure Dominique would call her sharply back. They stopped eventually, where a second path intersected the main one, beside a children's playground, deserted now. Thierry squinted at the sky and took a pack of cigarettes out of the breast pocket of his leather jacket. With his long fingers, he carefully removed two cigarettes, put them in his mouth, lit both, and handed one to Dominique. She scolded him, not for smoking, apparently, but for failing to offer one to Hannah. "Eh—*désolé.*" With no apparent irony, he proffered the pack to Hannah, who shook her head too quickly, gesticulating and laughing in a panicked, Jan-like manner, "Oh—no! *Non, merci!*" The two of them sat down on a bench to smoke. Hannah perched on the next one along, swinging her legs, looking at the sky, examining her nails. When they finished their cigarettes, they cozied into each other, sitting as close together as was physically possible, petite Dominique wrapped in Thierry's lanky body.

"Oh, look! A playground!" Hannah went to inspect it. She tried the slide, mugging clownishly and waving when Dominique and Thierry looked her way. Climbing up its stairs for a second time, she glanced at them. Dominique had turned fully into Thierry; they were in each other's arms, their mouths locked together. Whenever Hannah glanced at them after that, they were blatantly making out, and she had no choice but to keep busy and reanimate her expression—pretend interest in how the swing attached to the swing-set frame, what the climbing equipment was made of. It was so tedious she felt like crying. At last, the two of them stood up, and Dominique, for once speaking French, called abruptly, *"On y va, 'Annah!"*

At the highway underpass, she stood on her toes to kiss him goodbye, but somberly, nothing like the snickering you sometimes overheard at the end of the Lincoln dances when the dads driving the carpools pulled up. Dominique was silent as they walked the few blocks to her apartment. She looked unhappy, then her pinched little face seemed to settle into resignation. When they turned the corner onto her street, she swore. "*Zut,* I forget to buy the bread."

"You for*got,*" Hannah tried cheerfully, but Dominique gave her a blank look and set off at a rapid clip. They raced the two blocks to the store, Hannah pounding heavily beside

Dominique. The bread she bought was a baguette; Dominique said, *"Bonsoir, Madame,"* to the checkout lady, and the lady said, *"Bonsoir, Mesdemoiselles"* back—oh, there was so much to tell Jan already. Hannah should write a postcard this very night! *You'll never believe what we had for lunch on the first day. We had the funniest misunderstanding…* She did not write, however. She sent one postcard home the whole time, from the trip up to Normandy, and that because the Mesdames required it and provided everyone with stamped images of either Mont. St. Michel or Omaha Beach—until the boys made a run on the latter and there was no choice left. (*I'm having an amazing time!* Hannah wrote on the back of the picture of the ancient, isolated abbey. *Dominique is quite the character! Her family is so nice…and, needless to say, the chocolate is amazing!!! Tonight we are eating in a crêpe restaurant—une crêperie! I can't wait! Give Dottie a cuddle for me.*) It arrived after Hannah got home. It was she who fetched the mail out of the mailbox that day. She read it over, and the tone made her want to vomit, but it was too late; before she knew it, Jan had stuck it to the fridge—with the Eiffel Tower magnet Hannah had bought for her father in the airport—where it stayed for thirty years.

Back with the bread, in the long, brightly lit lobby of her building, Dominique withdrew a compact from her purse as they awaited the elevator, put her finger to her mouth, and rubbed something off her teeth. "Tomorrow," she said to her reflection in the little mirror, "'e bring a friend for you."

In Notre-Dame, where Hannah put a coin in a slot and lit a candle for her grandmother, Libby Turner awkwardly held hands with Marty Biddle, whom she towered over.

At the Louvre, Byron Suh jostled through the crowd before the painting they tried very hard to call *La Joconde* to slip his arm around Emmy Duke—and kept it there. Fred and Wendy Waxman were always finding excuses to touch each other—a fly in her hair, a smudge on his cheek. In the Bois de Boulogne, they lagged so far behind that Madame Dumas had to double back for them while Madame Giraud led the others on to the rose gardens no one any longer wanted to see.

On the *bâteau-mouche* down the Seine, as the others counted the bridges they went under, Hilary Thompkins extracted an admission from Libby's twin, Bruce, that the boys had a note-book ranking all of the girls—not just the girls on the trip but all of the Country Day girls they knew and even the French *corre-spondantes*. Byron Suh kept it hidden on his person. Then it was time to leave on the bus for the overnight trip to Normandy.

It was known—passed down from class eight to class eight—that *les mesdames* always retired early on the night of that trip, that as long as you kept it quiet, they would allow congregating in the rooms at the old *grange* in the coastal town. When the bus stopped at the American cemetery at Omaha Beach, everyone was slow to disembark—they were all clustered around Fred and Marty's seat as Marty unzipped his backpack a few inches to show the tops of the two bottles of hard cider he had sneaked into it. "We're gonna get more."

"It's illegal!" said Emmy Duke mildly.

"It's not illegal," Marty said with maximal scorn. "Are you a fucking idiot?"

Emmy smiled her dimply smile. "Well, it's sort of illegal."

Even the Lincoln boys walked soberly along the rows of white crosses, as if here, at last, was tourism they could approve of.

"What an incredible color," said Catherine when they stood on the sand looking down at the blue-green sea. "It's almost opaque." Nodding irritably, Hannah determined that she would not get stuck behind in the girls' bunk room with Catherine that night—she would cozy up to Wendy and Libby and Jessica. But in the event, she headed back across the hall well before the other girls who gathered in the boys' room after lights-out. After all of the speculation, the most obvious—the most clichéd—thing imaginable had happened, had been happening, and now was confirmed: Fred Standish had gone with Wendy Waxman. The lack of imagination drove Hannah crazy. It wasn't that she'd thought she herself had a chance with Fred—not really—but she was fond of the narrative where Jessica or Libby or someone a tiny bit less obvious came up trumps.

The boys had not managed to buy more cider. They had mostly hogged it—starting in before dinner, at which they played loudly at drunkenness. The second bottle was passed around the room and the girls, sitting on the bottom bunks or in twosomes on the floor, given tastes. "This is nothing," Libby said witheringly. "I've been ordering it all week. I didn't even know it was alcoholic. It's not like a gin and tonic."

Hannah assumed the evening would, at the minimum, advance toward spin the bottle. But it quickly devolved into a protracted drama of the girls trying to get the notebook off the boys. "Well, if you won't show it to us, then just tell us our numbers!" Wendy wheedled coyly. "Tell us our individual ranking!" Which was irritating, Hannah thought, for Wendy would never be lower than two or three.

"Yeah, tell us where we are!" said Jessica. "We don't care."

"Guys, let's do something else!" This was Hilary Thompkins,

who strode restlessly around the room, sometimes pausing to gaze out the window, perhaps missing ski racing.

"Yeah, come on, this is boring." Hannah glanced gratefully at Byron Suh, impressed he would take a stand, but Wendy was fixated. She seemed to have some challenge going with Marty even though she wasn't with him, she was with Fred. They taunted each other nonstop—had a running, equally tiresome game going of stealing and hiding each other's things. Hannah, sensing her own extreme irrelevance, suddenly couldn't tolerate sitting there any longer. Funny, when she would have given her scholarship to Country Day to sit in this room a week ago. She got up off the floor and went to bed, surprising the other girls, she could see; trying something out for the first time—making herself scarce.

"Was it fun?" asked Catherine quickly from her bunk when Hannah creaked open the door.

"Nah. It was so boring." She closed the door behind her. "You didn't miss anything," she said, belatedly finding a loyalty to the serious girl that ended up lasting longer than the postcard on her parents' fridge.

The friend Thierry brought with him was half a head shorter than he was and more sturdily built—stocky, you could even say—with pale hair. For half a minute Hannah was disappointed, having pictured herself with a Thierry double. Then she didn't care. *'E bring a friend for you.* He was called Robert. "Roh-bear," Hannah heard. "Oh! Robert!" she said belatedly, pronouncing it the American way, and though Dominique's and Thierry's faces remained neutral, not seeing the humor, the boy himself laughed. He inspected her closely then, studying her face as if to know what she was really about—was it delight that was hiding somewhere behind his eyes? "Yes! Tees de same name! Roe-*bett! Roe*-bett!"

She had never had a boy look at her that way, nor would she again for years, not in high school or college, not through all the fumbling hookups and the false starts and the sex and the drunkenness. Not even her first—call it starter—husband looked at her that way, though there would be others. All along there were always others, whether the interval was a month or a decade. You didn't forget. There was the visiting colleague's husband at the dinner party up in Washington Heights on the rainy night; the grad student from Berkeley interviewing for the postdoc. No, you didn't forget. It was like after the visit to Sacré-Coeur, when she was sitting for the caricaturist, feeling self-conscious—exposed and not pretty enough—and she felt the artist's gaze on her face, the performative salesmanship fallen away as he sized up the essential elements that made up her character. Marty Biddle, the class clown, standing behind the man's seat watching him draw, looked from the picture to Hannah and back again and said ruefully, "Hers is the best."

They walked the same way through the wooded park; they sat on the same benches. Halfway there, Robert took her arm, then her hand, enlacing her fingers with his. She was shocked by the connection—the intimacy of it. It was as if her whole body fell away, leaving only the hand, as they continued on through the park. She flushed and had to swallow. They spoke minimally as they walked along. *Where do you come from? How long you stay in Paris?* When Hannah switched to French, he went along with it, seeming neither relieved nor offended. He got more loquacious, explaining something about his brother versus himself—something about car-racing? His face in profile was chipper, puppyish. They were drawing near the children's playground. Hannah felt hot in her coat; she swallowed again. Either he liked car-racing and his brother did not or vice versa. She couldn't think straight and understood only stray phrases. Then they were on the bench—their own bench. *'E bring a friend for you.* Instead of pulling her toward him, as she had imagined he would (and "he" had taken many forms, from Prince Andrew to Fred Standish), he looked at her again and chucked his chin up ever so slightly—a cue! she realized—so that she leaned into him as if she knew what she was doing. Belatedly she had heard his name for the American name that it also was. Belatedly she opened her mouth—why, she'd had no idea! *French-kissing.* All those slumber parties where they told dildo jokes and fucked Fred Standish. No one had thought to mention that the boy's tongue went in your mouth? It was disgusting. No—it was everything. Presently, Roh-bear took the hand that was resting lightly on her side and put it behind her head, pushing his fingers into her thick hair. She pulled away—some instinct made her. Instantly, she regretted it—so much so, she could have burst out crying, like a baby. She wondered how she would get him to kiss her again. She laughed, said nervously in French, "Madame tells me my hair is *châtain-clair.*" Raising his gaze to above her forehead, Roh-bear considered this. He pulled one strand free and brought it forward into the light, making an unhurried study. *"Ouais."* He nodded finally. *"Je suis d'accord. Châtain-clair."* He gave a little tug on today's headband—black velvet—before letting it settle back into place. "What you call this?"

"Headband," she said. "Head. Band. Band for the head."

*   *   *

This exchange is what Hannah thinks of on the bus going back down to Paris from Normandy when she finds out that she is just above average in the rankings of the Lincoln boys' notebook. Top half, anyway. She'll take it. Clotilde—Wendy's *correspondante*—with a face like a supermodel's, is at the top of the list, and, though any girl in their class who could have chosen what to look like would have chosen, without one second's hesitation, Wendy Waxman—compact and boyish, with neat symmetrical features and a body that had nothing whatever at stake—Emmy Duke is on top of the American girls, breasts so big they look a burden, slowing her down in field hockey and basketball, requiring bras like medical apparatuses. It's as if Emmy Duke has understood her ranking intuitively for years— that placid, un-offendable smile. On the bus trip home, the *mesdames* find out about the boys' book and demand that they turn it over. Madame Giraud stows it in her handbag. The boys are dressed down but not with any particular venom. When they stop at a gas station to refuel, Hannah notices Madame Giraud casting her eye down the list with a frown on her face as if she, too, disagrees with the order and would make corrective marks if she could.

In April, the day after the *correspondants/-dantes* arrive in Boston, there is a big party at the Turners' grand gray house in Pembridge with the white Corinthian columns out front—just like La Madeleine, observes Catherine. Hannah doesn't answer and sulks through the party. She missed the much-ballyhooed reception at Logan Airport the day before because Dominique

Lefebvre, in the end, doesn't come. Hannah's *correspondante*, alone out of all of the French girls and boys, has declined to take part in the second half of the exchange. Hannah, afraid of being late, is the first to arrive at the party. The other parents come to drop off their children and are invited in for a drink on the fly—even Catherine's father, the ponderous Professor Beier, is coaxed into staying. Hannah, not realizing this would be the case, instructed her father not to get out of the car, not even to turn down the Turners' long gravel driveway. Not wanting to do the hour-plus round trip twice from Musketaquid, Mr. Beale goes and waits in the parking lot of the Howard Johnson's by the traffic circle.

The Country Day girls hope there will be many more joint activities with the boys. They fret as they put their coats on at the end of the party, lingering—stalling—not wanting it to be over. "Isn't anyone else planning anything for the whole group?" But no one is. They will have to wait till the May dance to see their own boys again, and at that point, they worry, the French-trip connections will have weakened as the boys pay attention to girls they haven't spent hours on a bus with—seen nodding off, teeth unbrushed, on overnight flights.

The remaining U.S. outings were for the girls only. The Tedeschis, who owned a chain of dry cleaners, took them to an amusement park where Wendy's *correspondante*, Clotilde, threw up on the roller-coaster ride. "Jesus," said Libby in disgust. "What would she do on the Green Serpent?" Emmy Duke's mother procured tickets to the Boston Ballet. Beforehand, they rode on the Swan Boats in the Public Garden. The French girls delighted in throwing peanuts into the river—all except

Clotilde, who was queasy. Hannah sat beside her, babysitting her. She shook her head grimly when Wendy asked, "You sure you don't mind?"

Hannah had found out that Dominique wasn't coming not from her but from Madame Giraud after they were home. Alone, she went through the planned activities with a raw feeling of injustice, as if Dominique's failing to come was a rejection of her, her parents, her house, which was so far from Pembridge, of her life on the fringes as a non-Kate, as a two-year-girl who'd barely squeaked in right at the end. For, somehow, she knew it wasn't simply the logistical problem Madame Giraud had claimed the Lefebvres had. It wasn't until years later that Hannah understood that it wasn't just the money either, although it might have been. She, of all people, ought to have understood. It was a class issue. Dominique's life didn't allow for leaving her parents and larking off to the United States for adventures and treats. It wasn't that she wouldn't have enjoyed it, though that was probably true as well. It wasn't merely that she didn't have time, with her "big dance," her big audition to prepare for. It was that it didn't enter into her considerations— it wasn't a part of her life and never would be. The Lefebvres must have gone out on a limb, signing up to have Hannah come. Her visit, perhaps, had been an anomalous attempt on the part of Dominique's mother to mainstream her child, let her have the kind of fun other girls had. When she got older, Hannah sometimes pictured Dominique as one of those people who say, "I'd like to visit New Mexico," and do just that—once, say, for a week, with the boyfriend of the moment, and come home enthused about the desert sky and southwestern flora, with no pretension of doing more or organizing their travel in a top-down manner reflecting a widely accepted hierarchy of touristic priorities.

Mrs. Peter Duke the program for the Boston Ballet's *La Bayadère* said under the list of Gold Star sponsors. What that meant was that the girls could go backstage afterward; they could meet the ballerinas—not the famous soloist, but a couple of members of the corps de ballet whose flowing yet highly synchronized dances were Hannah's favorite part. It fascinated her to see, as they mingled with the two young women, still in their softly elegant costumes of satin and tulle, and took turns posing for pictures with them, that up close, these most exquisite ballerinas, these visions of femininity and grace, did not necessarily have beautiful faces. In fact, the one Hannah posed with was quite ugly, with a low heavy brow and painful acne scars on her cheeks. Ballet wasn't, after all, going to be the realm of the Holly Hobbies—of Emmy Duke herself, for instance, whose mother encouraged her to take up fifth position beside the ballerina for a photograph. On an impulse Hannah bought a postcard in the lobby and sent it off to 22, rue du Moulin, writing in English as she knew Dominique would prefer. *We saw an amazing* Bayadère *this afternoon. I thought of you! Hope you pass the audition!*

Dominique never wrote back. Hannah had not expected her to—a reply would have been so out of character as to be disappointing. But Hannah knew now that what she had claimed on the steps of La Madeleine was true—Dominique Lefebvre would make it as a dancer. The melancholy she felt on the outings lifted. Now she had her discernment to keep her company.

As for Roh-bear, he did write to her—not once but twice! Hannah destroyed the postcards, not only to hide them from Jan but also because she was unwilling to try to reconcile the embarrassingly stilted prose with the walk in the park, with a second occasion when the two of them had hung out by themselves, eating chocolate in a square near Dominique's apartment—chocolate that he had kissed off of her fingers, embarrassing her, then making her feel annoyed at herself that she was embarrassed. What could she tell him? That word had gotten out among the girls and trickled down to the boys that Hannah Beale had a French boyfriend? That because of this, she felt Fred Standish's eyes on her at the Turners' party, that he'd sought her out, confided in her, then told her at the May dance, when, truthfully, she found it rather boring, that she was the only one who actually understood him? Should she have told him that she thought of him in the moment that Marty Biddle made a beeline across the gym to her as "Stairway to Heaven" started, the slow dance that closed every Lincoln dance? Acceptable she was now, apparently—she would have thanked him if she could have.

The coffee is winding down. Privately, Hannah has admired the way Dana steered the conversation around to the ask itself. Hannah is an easy touch—when Dana names a number, she agrees to it without a murmur. In these tech-boom years, she knows the amount is exceedingly modest by comparison, but Dana seems pleased—maybe even surprised. Participation, she assures Hannah, is what it's all about. As they stand up, buttoning on their coats, joking about having had too much caffeine today, the young woman finds a generosity, perhaps in return for Hannah's acquiescence to "the number," which maybe isn't too bad for a college prof married to a surgeon: "It sounds like you had a good time on that French trip," she allows.

This is Hannah's cue to be distant, to be corporate, to be appropriate. But as they push through the doors into the cold spring air, she says, as if talking to a real friend, "The way they matched us up with the host-students was hilarious—I mean, if you look at it today."

"Oh, yeah?" The sun is waning, and they both pull their coats tighter around themselves.

"Everyone had their match."

"Okay. Interesting."

"The smartest girl in our class, Catherine Beier—the professor's daughter—well, her host family owned a bookstore." Hannah turns up one palm, then the other, setting up the joke. "Intellectual with intellectuals."

"Right, right…"

"And the prettiest, most popular girl, Wendy Waxman, got the prettiest, most popular *correspondante*. Now, *that* may have been by chance," Hannah concedes. "But knowing Madame Giraud…probably not!" At the suggestion that physical attractiveness is quantifiable, a look of mild alarm has crept over Dana's face. "And I? I got matched up with a poor girl!" When Dana doesn't seem to understand, Hannah elaborates. "Because I was on financial aid! They put the two poor kids together!"

She should have known better. As seems to happen more and more to Hannah, the young woman rushes to commiseration when what was wanted was laughter.

"What? *No.*"

Hannah supplies the laughter herself. "Kid you not."

"Oh my God! How awful!"

"Gotta love the eighties, right?"

In the weak urban sunlight, Dana winces. The junior development officer of Pembridge Country Day is empathetic—as it sinks in, she is scandalized. "That's so, so wrong, I can't even..." She is momentarily at a loss for words. "I assure you that that would *never* happen today. *All* of our students at PCD are made to feel that they one hundred percent belong on the same playing field as all other students. Financial-aid status has *no bearing*. No one would ever, I mean, ever...no student would ever—"

The repudiation goes on for so long that eventually Hannah realizes that what Dana actually is is embarrassed by the subject. Perhaps it's the last taboo—not the financial aid itself but the idea that it once entailed something. Not a quid pro quo but an understanding, anyway, that something was being given, something gotten. It never occurred to Hannah to be insulted by the premise—if anything, it made her feel less beholden to the place.

Or perhaps it's personal for Dana—"public school all the way"—imagining herself in Hannah's unattractive shoes with her scarlet letter of financial need, so many years ago. And perhaps, too, underneath the professed excitement, there's an unpleasant, unacknowledged truth of what it is like to work with this student body today, with this parent body, making—what? Forty thousand dollars a year?—as the junior development officer of Pembridge Country Day School, when the venture-cap money has come to town. Dana stops protesting at last, her face turned in Hannah's direction, yes, but her eyes half closed as she shakes her head as if to forbid this gross unfairness from entering in. "I'm just so sorry," she repeats when Hannah doesn't rush to corroborate the emotion—when Hannah fails to respond that she, of all people, is relieved to hear that no current student would ever be classified according to financial-aid status, when she fails to express her deep gratitude that the playing field has at last been evened out where it never was before.

Acknowledgments

I'd like to thank Angélique Dupichot, Alina Rocha Menocal, and Laura Kiernan for help with languages and settings; Shruti Sheth; and Tracy Roe. To thank Cressida Connolly once again may seem rote; her advice on these stories was anything but.

About the Author

CAITLIN MACY is the author of *Mrs.*, *The Fundamentals of Play*, and *Spoiled* and the recipient of an O. Henry Award. Her work has appeared in *The New Yorker* and the *New York Times Magazine*, among other publications. She lives in New York City with her husband and two children.